"What do you want to do at the new house?"

She laughed and tugged at her haphazard bun. "So much. A complete overhaul." When she looked up, he was staring at her with a look akin to awe.

"Santo? Are you okay?"

He nodded. "Uh…yes." His gaze moved over her face and then settled on her hair. "I've just never known a contractor with such beautiful hair."

A blush moved down Davina's neck. Great. Now she'd get the blotchies, as her sister Tilly always called them. A flush that only showed off her freckles. Maybe he wouldn't notice.

He kept staring at her.

"Santo, the house?"

"Oh, yes, the house," he said with a wry smile. "I need to focus on the house."

Frantic now, she searched her notes. What was happening to her anyway? She never acted like a ninny with clients.

With over seventy books published and millions in print, **Lenora Worth** writes award-winning romance and romantic suspense. Three of her books finaled in the ACFW Carol Awards, and her Love Inspired Suspense novel *Body of Evidence* became a *New York Times* bestseller. Her novella in *Mistletoe Kisses* made her a *USA TODAY* bestselling author. Lenora goes on adventures with her retired husband, Don, and enjoys reading, baking and shopping… especially shoe shopping.

Visit the Author Profile page at Harlequin.com for more titles.

Her
Lakeside Family

Lenora Worth

HARLEQUIN® LOVE INSPIRED®

LOVE INSPIRED BOOKS

Recycling programs
for this product may
not exist in your area.

ISBN-13: 978-0-373-89911-1

Her Lakeside Family

Therefore with joy shall ye draw water
out of the wells of salvation.
—*Isaiah* 12:3

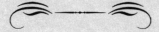

To my family, always.

Chapter One

"Lucia, stop aggravating your sister! Adriana, hurry and get your backpack. Daddy's late for work. And where did your brother go?"

A screaming cyclone whizzed by, all dark curls and giggles.

Nate.

Santo Alvanetti grabbed his two-year-old son and tried for the third time to get his shoes on. But Nate wasn't in the mood to get dressed so he kept running away, taking off an article of clothing each time. Now he was down to his little blue jeans and one shoe.

"Daddy, the school bus is coming," Lucia—the oldest, who'd just turned nine—screamed from the floor-to-ceiling front windows. "I'm gonna miss it again."

Santo sent her a pleading glance. "It's okay, honey. I'll drop you off at school."

The school was in town, near Millbrook Lake. Completely out of his way but he was already late. Thirty more minutes wouldn't hurt. His cell rang, indicating his being late had already cost him money. Alvanetti Imports moved at a fast pace. He needed to do the same, but these days every morning had become a challenge and a race against time.

Adriana stomped a booted foot. "I can't find my purse, Daddy."

"She has a purse?" he asked Lucia. His middle child was only seven. But then, her late mother had loved expensive purses.

Lucia's dark eyes opened wide. "Duh. We both do. Mom bought them for us a long time ago, before…" Her eyes went dull. "We need Mom back here. She knows how to find purses."

Santo wasn't sure how to answer that. His wife Althea was dead. She'd died a horrible death about a year ago, in a showdown with his sister Rikki and a police detective. While Santo both mourned her and resented her for betraying him, her children still missed her. Althea had tried to be a good mother but something had gone so wrong in their marriage.

Raising three children and trying to run a business made Santo too tired and stressed to try to figure out what had happened to bring his life crashing down around him. He thought of happier times with Althea, when they were younger and she still loved him. He'd pushed away his anger and pain for a while now, but his children had been acting out. They all needed help.

Nate started crying.

Santo wanted to cry right along with him but he couldn't do that. He had to be strong. He had to get to work. He needed every ounce of strength just to make it through each day. The import business the Alvanetti family had been running for decades was legitimate now and finally back in the black.

Because he'd put every waking hour into making it work.

So he grabbed Nate again and managed to get him dressed, but the boy didn't want to go to the day care.

"I want Mommy," the little boy cried, kicking to get out of Santo's arms.

Nate probably didn't remember Althea all that much but he always echoed whatever his older sisters said. The counselor had warned Santo to let his children talk about their mother but each time they mentioned her, his heart hurt with a pain that rivaled a jagged cut. It was a tear that would never heal. Promising himself he'd never go through that kind of pain again, Santo gritted his teeth and focused on his children.

The doorbell rang, the chimes echoing over the fifteen-foot-high ceiling and the modern, wood-and-steel open staircase. Outside the spring sunshine glistened on the infinity pool and the bay below the bluffs. Santo had a stunning view thanks to the wall of glass across from the living room and kitchen.

There had been a wall of glass between him and Althea, too.

But he didn't even notice the view anymore and the guilt he'd felt at not knocking down that wall between them had long dissipated like a morning mist over the water. He'd be so glad to get out of this house. Too many bad memories for him and too many memories of her for his children. They all needed a fresh start.

"Daddy, the bus!"

"Daddy, the doorbell!"

"I want Mommy."

He prayed the new nanny—one of many his sister, Rikki, had hired since Althea's death—had arrived. He hadn't met the woman but Rikki and Blain had vetted and cleared her, stating she had impeccable credentials. Santo hurried to the door and opened it while he held

Nate's squirming, screaming little body against his heart.

The woman standing there didn't look like the typical nanny. She had strawberry-blond hair that shot out in chunky layers around her face and chin. Her eyes were an ethereal green, like the bay waters in the early morning. She wore a plaid button-up shirt, worn jeans and… work boots.

"Hello," the woman said. "I'm—"

"I'm so glad you're here, Mrs. Brownlee," Santo interrupted, shoving Nate into her arms. "The instructions are on the counter in the kitchen. The girls go to Millbrook Elementary and they usually catch the bus or ride home with a neighbor. I'll take them to school and call the neighbor to pick them up this afternoon. Nate has day care but now that you're here, let's just keep him home today."

He kissed his sobbing son. "C'mon, girls."

Nate started crying all over again. But the woman standing there marched right on in and said something soothing in his son's ear. Nate hiccupped and stopped crying, his misty brown eyes glued on the woman holding him.

She smiled over at Santo. "I'm sorry but—"

"I want my purse," Adriana said on a scream, her long brown curls falling over her purple tunic and matching leggings. She looked at the surprised woman. "I can't leave without my purse."

The pretty nanny looked at Adriana with sympathetic eyes. "Of course not. I never leave home without my—"

"Found it," Lucia said, shoving the shiny purple shoulder bag at her little sister. "Now can I please get to school?"

Santo let out a sigh and nodded to the woman. "You don't have to apologize but please try to be on time from now on, okay?"

The woman's green eyes flared with something akin to mirth. "Mr. Alvanetti, I don't think you understand. I'm not—"

"I'm here." A shrill, laughing voice came from the open door. "And not a moment too soon from the looks of things."

Confused, Santo turned to find a plump, smiling woman with short auburn hair and black-framed, crystal-encrusted glasses standing on the threshold. "I'm Virginia Brownlee. I'm your nanny."

Santo looked from the smiling woman at the door to the bemused woman still holding his son. "Then who are you?"

"I've been trying to tell you that for the last five minutes," she said, passing Nate back to him. "I'm Davina Connell. I'm here to help you get this house in shape to sell. I'm the contractor."

Davina almost felt sorry for him.

Santo Alvanetti exuded power and assurance, his tailor-made suit, his hair crisp and dark and falling in touchable curls around his face and neck much in the same way as his son's. But right now, the man's expression filled with realization and panic, his onyx gaze darkening even more.

"I am so sorry," he said, obviously rewinding his thoughts so he could assess the situation. "It's been one of those mornings and I was expecting Mrs. Brownlee and I must have gotten the time wrong and…I completely forgot you would be coming by today."

Even as he explained, one of the beautiful little girls let out a yelp and his son started crying again. While his cell buzzed over and over.

"Give me the boy," Mrs. Brownlee said in a manner that made them all stop what they were doing. "I'll put him in his car seat and I'll get the girls to school. You did alert the school that I have permission to drop them off and pick them up, of course."

His gaze moved from the prim woman to Davina. "Not yet, but I'll put that on my list."

"Well, let's get on with it then," Mrs. Brownlee said, her big glasses and boot-cut jeans made her look much too hip to be a nanny.

"Look, I'll drop the girls at school," he replied. "And I'll get it all straightened out. If you can just handle Nate."

"Nate and I will be fine," Mrs. Brownlee replied. "When you get home tonight, I'll go over the terms of my employment. For now, we're all going to be okay."

He looked from her to Davina again as if caught in a trap. Again, Davina felt empathy and sympathy for him, her heart doing a little tug that made her much too aware of how handsome the man was. "Would you walk me to my car?" he asked. "So we can discuss what needs to be done with the house?"

"Sure." Davina smiled at Mrs. Brownlee, her heart hammering an erratic beat against her insides. "I'll be back to look over the house and do some calculating, if that's okay with both of you."

Mrs. Brownlee nodded. "Won't bother me a bit." Giving them both an impish grin, she added, "I'll be doing the same."

"Let's go, girls," he said, prodding the two dark-haired children toward his sleek sedan.

After he had the chattering, fussing girls inside the car with their seat belts on, he left the driver's door open and turned to Davina. "I'm so sorry I didn't know who you were. I thought my sister said David…somebody…would be coming by. I wasn't expecting—"

"A woman?" she finished. "I've never been called David but my dad calls me Dani." She spelled out the nickname for him. "I prefer Davina, however."

"Davina," he said, his dark eyes pouring over her like liquid chocolate. "I think I'll remember your name from now on."

"It's okay," she said to hide the sizzle of something richer and darker than even his chocolate eyes. "I was hoping we could do a walk-through on the house."

His cell buzzed with an annoying hum. "Work," he explained, checking it and shutting it down. "I'm late for a meeting."

And by the way he was fidgeting, he wanted out of here.

"Well, I'm burning daylight," she said in her firm voice that usually made surprised, unsure men sit up and take notice. "What do you want me to do?"

"Rikki trusts you so I guess I will, too," he replied, already getting into the car. "Look it over and call me with an estimate. Maybe we can meet here again later."

"Maybe." She wasn't going to hold her breath on that. "My time is just as valuable as yours, so that's your choice."

He stared up at her again, causing Davina to shiver even while the early springtime sun was warm on her skin. "My sister says you come highly recommended," he said. "She just neglected to explain that you're a woman."

"Does that matter?" Davina asked, used to this type of conversation. "I work harder than any man you could hire." She handed him her business card.

"It matters," he said, his tone low and gravelly. Tucking the card in his pocket, he added, "But not in the way you might think."

Then he cranked the car and backed out of the driveway, leaving Davina to wonder why her being here should matter to him at all.

Chapter Two

Davina moved around the modern, sleek living room of the house on the bay, reminding herself she was taking on this job and the renovation of the other house this man had also purchased because her friend Rikki Alvanetti Kent had handpicked her. She'd known Rikki since college and they'd kept up with each other since they both worked in the same field.

Rikki was an interior designer, so they threw each other work here and there. And this was a big chunk of work.

Davina needed this project on her résumé since she was trying to establish her budding construction company as a leading player in the ever-changing Southern real estate market. But she'd heard the rumors that swirled with all the flickering evasiveness of fireflies around the quaint town of Millbrook Lake, Florida.

Santo Alvanetti came from a gangster family. A Mafia lord. His wife murdered two people close to Rikki Alvanetti and tried to kill her, too. Althea Alvanetti died in a shoot-out at an old warehouse. Detective Blain Kent killed her to save the woman he loved. The whole mess involved a diamond-and-emerald necklace that belonged to Santo's mother, Sonia.

Everyone says they've changed and that they aren't doing anything illegal now, but you need to stay away from that family.

Although she and Rikki hadn't talked in detail about the tragedy that had happened over a year ago, Rikki had told her if she didn't feel comfortable taking the job, they'd all understand. But Davina had a policy that had always served her well. Ignore the rumors and get to the truth. And in renovating houses, the truth always lay in the bones. This house was a showpiece, no doubt. But the bones were sorely lacking.

Something was missing.

"I don't feel the love," Mrs. Brownlee said as she came back into the big open area with the majestic windows that highlighted the pool and the water beyond. "I just don't feel it at all."

Davina turned toward the older woman. "Me either. There's a sadness shadowing this brilliant room."

"I think it's called neglect," Mrs. Brownlee replied, running her finger over a dusty table, her earrings swaying. "It lacks warmth."

"Yes, I agree," Davina said. She liked Virginia Brownlee. "Even with the stunning view and all the glass that brings in the sunshine, it's still a bit cold."

"Call me Virginia," the other woman said. "What do you aim to do to make this place worthy of love again?"

Davina grinned and grabbed the leather tool pouch her daddy had given her for her twenty-fifth birthday. Da had always understood her need to hammer and build since he'd once owned his own construction company. A company where she'd worked after school and on weekends just to learn the business. Until her daddy had booted her out and sent her on her way once she'd finished college.

Now, she turned to study Virginia Brownlee. "You're awfully blunt. I like that."

"I don't pull any punches," Virginia replied, her brown eyes turning melancholy. "This family is in crisis. But I knew that coming in. Such a tragedy."

Davina wasn't going to gossip.

"But it's not my place to discuss Mr. Alvanetti's personal life with anyone," Virginia replied, confirming that she didn't intend to do that either. Lowering her voice, she added, "My focus is on the children. I'm going to check on little Nathan. I think he might be coming down with something."

"Have you always been a nanny?" Davina asked, making conversation since they'd be around each other a lot during the next few weeks.

"No." Her new friend started up the open stairs and unlocked the safety gate at the top.

Okay, a bit cryptic but maybe the woman didn't like nosy questions. Davina was known for asking a lot of questions, however. Curiosity could get her into trouble.

"I'll be measuring and taking notes," Davina replied in a loud retort. "I'll also have my crew come back with me later to show them what needs to be done. I think I can bring this place up to speed to sell but it'll be a challenge."

"And bring the light back into this home," Virginia said with a smile, her hoop earrings jangling. Then she toddled off on her cushioned wedge loafers, her funky glasses sparkling in the sun.

Mary Poppins with Bohemian earrings is in the house, Davina thought. But this house needed someone to shake it up if Santo expected to get top dollar when he put it on the market. Davina moved around the wide rectangular kitchen, ideas popping into her head. The planes and angles of this place were sharp and jagged, made of wood, stone and granite. Icy. Cold. Unyielding.

Like the man who owned it?

His eyes weren't icy. They were rich and warm and chocolate. She loved chocolate. Especially dark chocolate. But his onyx gaze also held a hint of regret and a longing for redemption.

Stop that, she cautioned. *Out of your league. Out of your range. Not your type at all.*

Davina wasn't sure what her type was anyway, since she went through what her younger sister, Tilly, called *possibles* as fast as she went through nails. She didn't have time to date, let alone think about a client in romantic terms. Her chaotic family back in Bayou Fontaine, a sleepy river town near New Orleans, needed her help.

Her brother Darren, a hothead who thought he should be ahead of his baby sister in the construction field, always teased her about her pointed views and blunt ways.

"You can't be mushy and sentimental about building houses, Davina. You'll never survive."

She'd not only survived. She'd thrived. She didn't build houses. She rebuilt them. Her daddy had forced her out of the company, telling her she needed to make her own way. Now her overconfident brother wasn't speaking to her but that was okay. As long as Darren took care of what was left of Connell Construction, she'd do her part by helping with the family finances.

So she ignored how Santo Alvanetti made her stomach lift and crash like a confused wave and started taking notes on what needed to be done to breathe some life into this stunning house.

Two hours later, the front door opened and Davina jumped and whirled around to find Santo standing there staring at her.

"I shouldn't have left like that," he said. "I hurried through my meeting so I could get back to you. I mean, back to this." He lifted a hand toward the high ceilings. "I need to get away from this house and I've put off doing it long enough. My children need a new start in a more modest, child-friendly home. Whatever you can do to make that happen, I'm all for it."

Davina went to her tote bag and pulled out a cupcake centered in a clear plastic container. "Breakfast," she said with a shrug. "But I'm willing to share. I never make decisions on an empty stomach and I got so involved in work, I forgot I had this in my bag."

Glancing at her cupcake, he said, "I know

where you bought that and I sure *hope* you're willing to share it."

"Let's go over my plans for this place and then…I might let you have half. That is if you agree to my stipulations."

"You're tough, aren't you?"

Davina wasn't all that tough. Right now, she felt weak, her knees trembled and her sturdy boots were the only thing holding her up. Santo Alvanetti seemed to be flirting with her. Probably trying to make up for that false start, which was still kind of sweet since she got to hold that adorable little boy.

"Don't look so glum," she said, trying to show him she could be fair. "I'll try to make this as painless as possible."

He actually smiled. And her insides turned as mushy as the center of this Peaches-and-Cream cupcake she'd bought earlier.

Mushy doesn't cut it, Davina.

The challenging echo of her brother's words made her spine stiffen. And made her want to demo something.

"From Marla's place?" Santo asked, hopefulness cresting in his expression when he pointed to the cupcake.

"Don't you know it," she retorted, trying to calm her suddenly jittery nerves. "We'll nibble while we walk and talk. I have a lot of ideas."

* * *

An hour later, Santo felt sick to his stomach, the sweet bite of cupcake weighing heavily against his gut. "This is your estimation?" Staring at the figures on her list of needed updates, he said, "I thought some paint and a few new rugs would do the trick."

"Then you don't know your house," she retorted, her black pen tapping the paper. "One of your toilets has a loose handle and really, the whole thing has seen better days. You need something with less water-flow. More economical."

"Toilets? I hadn't even thought of toilets."

"My point exactly."

"Okay, so you also listed new hardwood flooring to replace the tile in here?"

"Yes. To warm things up and make the floors more family-friendly for the next owners. This marble in the entryway from the pool is dangerous for children with wet feet. We can put a sturdy rug there to keep the skids to a minimum."

"And adults, too," he admitted. "I've slipped there myself, several times." Althea used to laugh at him when he'd wipe out. Of course, his deceased wife always walked around in stilettos.

"Then I think engineered wooden floors

with heavy rugs at all the entryways will help with that. Now, in the bedrooms we can go with a strong, durable allergy-free carpet for the kids' rooms and maybe hardwood in the master." She paused. "Oh, and your master shower is outdated and kind of pretentious."

He nodded and winced. "I've never liked it. I don't need a waterfall inside a terrarium running 24/7 near my shower."

"Good. Because this is a house, not a jungle," she said on a smile. Then she went on to explain several more problems that he'd either ignored or hadn't even been aware of. "We can fix all of it with a few tweaks and some sweat equity."

"I wish it could be a home again," he replied. "I'll write you a check for the renovations."

"I'm sorry for what you've had to deal with," she said on a low tone.

His radar went up and the trust stirring between them disappeared. "What have you heard?"

Davina's soft green gaze held his, strong and steady. "Enough," she said. "But I don't gossip and I don't judge. I'm just sorry for your loss and everything you and Rikki have been through. She told me a little but…it seemed hard for her to talk about so I didn't pressure her."

Santo exhaled a breath. No, he didn't like

to talk about this and furthermore she was an outsider who had no reason to be involved in the horror of his past. But maybe he could trust her.

"I lost more than my wife," he admitted. "Getting out of this house seems like the right thing to do. To start a new phase of my life with my children. I tried to make it work but instead of getting better, things are getting worse. It's not healthy. They need a different kind of home now." He leaned against the counter. "And I need to be away from this place."

"Well, that's where I come in," Davina replied, her tone thankfully neutral. "I'll fix this one up to sell and then we'll tackle the one you bought on the lake. Now that is going to be a charmer."

He wanted to tell her she was a charmer. She made him smile and Santo had forgotten how to do that. But he couldn't go on just a smile. He needed her to get this done so they could all get on with their lives. "I suppose it will be worth giving my children something new and hopeful to focus on. I'll cover the expenses. So do whatever you need to do. Just do it fast."

"It might take as long as three weeks here and at least that many months on the lake house. So my crew and I will be around for a while."

Santo wasn't sure he wanted to hear that, either. Strangers moving through his home at all hours. "Okay. I'll make arrangements to keep the kids out of your hair."

"I'll coordinate that with Mrs. Brownlee," she said. "I'll bring in a couple of crew members and we'll work around your routine."

Santo realized he was letting other people control his life these days but he didn't know how to get it back on track without a little help. His sister, Rikki, had taken over a lot of the responsibilities around here. Santo needed to get himself together so Rikki could enjoy her married life.

"Whatever you have to do to make this quick and painless, I'd appreciate," he said to Davina. "I'll be at work most of the time but I'll check in on things."

She stood across the counter, her gaze danced over him and then back to what remained her of the once-giant cupcake. "Okay, now we can work out the details about who gets the rest of that cupcake."

Santo laughed in spite of the heaviness that had burdened him for months now. "You've been eyeing that thing the whole time, haven't you?"

"I sure have," she said, grabbing the cupcake

holder. Then she launched back into her grand plan for his house.

Santo listened, watching as she nibbled on the cupcake without losing a crumb. In awe, he couldn't remember the last time he'd felt this relaxed, money and remodeling aside.

When she whirled around to face him, they almost crashed together but he caught her and then stood back, the second of contact jolting through him like an electric shock.

But Davina didn't miss a beat even if her eyes did widen. "And wait until you hear what I have in mind for the lake house. We'll have a whole cake to soften that blow when I go over the details."

Santo decided he could handle that. Davina was smart and talented and determined. And she loved her work. His sister had put him in good hands. But then, Rikki knew him so well and she'd been through this awful ordeal, too. He was glad she'd moved back here and he had grudgingly accepted her husband, Blain Kent, as a trusted friend. They'd both been a comfort to Santo over these last long months and truth be told, they'd suffered just as much as he had. Blain still had nightmares about having to shoot Santo's wife in order to save Rikki. But they had each other and Blain loved Rikki.

Santo wished he and Althea could have had that kind of solid foundation.

Maybe this house had been built on sinking sand.

He had no one, and his children, while a joy, weren't old enough to understand what he was dealing with. Not yet, but Lucia had asked a lot of questions.

He'd have to make good on his side of this bargain, Santo decided. He'd have to invest some sweat equity of his own.

And watching Davina now with anticipation lighting up her pretty face, he didn't think that would be such a hardship. She'd breathed new life into this house.

Maybe being around her could bring him back to life, too.

Chapter Three

Two days later, Davina stood in the galley kitchen of the garage apartment Rikki had suggested she rent for the spring. Since she'd be here in Millbrook Lake for months, Davina had readily agreed after seeing the neat little one-bedroom apartment located on the church grounds. It had a massive picture window with a great view of the lake, and she could walk to church and just about anywhere else. She loved walking around the lake every evening. Tonight would be a good time. Lovely, warm and with a gentle breeze.

But her cell rang before she could go put on her sneakers.

Mom.

"Hello," Davina said, waiting for the usual questions of "How are you? Are you working too hard? Are you seeing anyone?"

She got those and more, but she only told her mom what she wanted her to know. Coming from a big, noisy and nosy family had shaped Davina's entire personality. She liked being independent and out on her own, even if she did miss her family all the time. But she wasn't about to tell her mother about Santo Alvanetti.

"When are you gonna settle down?" Nancy asked each time she went home to Bayou Fontaine.

"I'm settled, Ma," Davina would always reply. "Settled into my work. I love what I do and one day, I'll finally get our house back the way it should be."

Ma always laughed and kissed her on the cheek. "Look at you, worrying about this old money trap when you need to be having babies and cooking meals."

She didn't want babies and meals. She wanted rooms to paint and trim and she wanted walls to tear down and rebuild. Her daddy had once been in charge of a growing construction company but his bad health and some equally bad decisions during the lean housing market had caused him to almost lose everything. She and Darren had done what they could, but Da was still working part-time and still struggling.

He'd forced Davina to leave the nest, telling

her she had a lot of talent that she shouldn't waste following him around.

But she'd always wondered if maybe her dad had sent her away because she was a woman and he believed she'd never be good at construction.

She'd show all of them. She wanted to help her family so she needed to get her crew settled in nearby apartments and hotels since they'd be here for the long haul.

Santo and his adorable children came to mind.

He had a family. A family in need of a good home. A loving home. But he also had walls that needed rebuilding. Or moving.

"You'll certainly have a challenge with *him*," she mumbled.

Santo Alvanetti had a solid wall around himself.

An invisible wall that he didn't even see and a wall he obviously couldn't see through, either. Davina always summed up a home owner while she was measuring and calculating. It didn't take much to sum up Santo Alvanetti. Widowed, tragic and stressed to the max. Unavailable. Unwilling to risk anything. With anyone.

Her focus was on getting his place in shape to sell so she could get to the really good project. The old rambling house he'd bought on the lake in town. That house had not only good bones. It had a real heart. It would be the one house that could showcase her talents on a regional and maybe even a national level.

Davina would focus on the houses and not their owner because her goal had always been on rebuilding and renovating.

Virginia would focus on the children.

But Davina had to wonder who was focusing on helping Santo Alvanetti to heal from his wife's betrayal.

"I can't seem to focus."

Santo didn't like admitting that but he had to talk to someone and the man sitting across from him was the only person he could trust not to spread any more rumors about him.

Rory Sanderson's blue eyes remained calm and blank. He was a good minister and Santo liked him a lot. But Rikki and her friends had brought him kicking and screaming to visit with the man who preached each Sunday at the Millbrook Lake Church in town. Today for the sake of privacy, Rory had driven the few miles north of town to the offices and warehouse at Alvanetti Imports to counsel Santo. While he looked more like a beach bum or maybe a surfer than a minister, Rory was kind and compassionate and he withheld judgment. He listened a lot more than he advised. Which scored points with Santo. He was so tired of unsolicited, unmanageable advice.

"Why can't I just snap out this?" he asked Rory now, his gaze moving to the business card on his desk that stated in a bold, black scroll—*Davina Connell Construction, Bayou Fontaine, Louisiana.* "I have a new nanny and she's great with the kids and Davina Connell is working day and night to update the house. It's beginning to look like a different place, a better place. She's doing things I would have never thought of doing. I should be able to relax a little and concentrate on what's important. I've never had trouble balancing things, even when Althea neglected the entire family. I made it work but now…I don't have any energy. I need to keep things going for my children and for this business."

"It takes time," Rory said. "Grief can take a toll and it shows up in many forms and it comes at the most unexpected times. It can exhaust you completely. You and the children might all experience outbursts, impatience, lack of focus, lack of appetite, lack of sleep."

"All of the above," Santo admitted. "I see the outbursts in my children but I know I lose my patience even more now than I did before."

"So you've never been a patient man?" Rory asked with a wry smile.

"Not very good at it, no." Santo thought back over the last year or so. "It's been a while since… Althea died. I thought I'd be able to get on with my life by now but I can see how this was building up when she was still alive. My children are still suffering and I don't know how to help them."

"You can help them by *learning* to be patient. But more importantly, you need to be in the moment with them. I know that might sound cliché, but it works," Rory replied on a gentle note. "Hold them. Talk to them. Sit with them. Read to them. And when they ask about their mother, let them talk and try to answer their questions."

"How can I explain what happened to my wife?" Santo asked, that old dread burning through his stomach. "I can't tell them the truth. It's hard enough for me to accept but to explain that she died because she was trying to steal from our family and she became a murderer—trying to explain that to my children is downright impossible."

"You don't need to give them the brutal details," Rory replied. "Not yet. But Lucia is old enough to hear things at school or even at church and you've mentioned she's already asked some questions. Other children can be cruel. You don't have to tell her anything but if she comes home upset, let her explain and then work from there. You can tell her that her mommy went through a bad time and made some bad choices and that you're sad she got into trouble. If your children ask for the truth, you have to keep reminding them that Althea loved them and that it's not their fault any of this happened."

Santo leaned over his desk, a hand going to his forehead. "I don't want that day to come, Rory. My heart can't take seeing my children hurting any more than they already are. That's why I decided to move. She came home crying one day because a friend teased her about not having a mom anymore."

"No one's heart is safe when it comes to their children," Rory said. "Parents hurt when their children hurt. But you have to be strong for them."

"I'm tired," Santo said. "Too tired."

"Have you thought about taking some time off?"

He let out a sigh and picked up a pen that had the Alvanetti logo on it. "I can't."

Rory didn't push him. "Well, maybe leave a little early once or twice a week. Surely you have someone here you can trust to run this place in your absence." Then Rory added an enticing tidbit of a suggestion. "Why don't you do what you said you'd do and help Davina and her crew with the renovations on the lake house?"

Santo thought about that. Was he afraid to turn over the reins to anyone else? Probably since his trust meter was broken these days. He'd certainly become more controlling since his wife's betrayal and death. "I did tell her I'd put in some sweat equity," he said. "But I'd probably get in the way."

"Davina's good at showing home owners how to become handymen," Rory said. "She was gentle with Vanessa and me when we renovated Vanessa's house. A word of warning, however. Davina believes in authenticity. The house is a Craftsman style and she made sure we both honored that."

Santo grinned and bobbed his head. "Yes, over the last couple of weeks, I've heard all about my mid-century modern and how I should have been true to that style while updating as needed. The woman is a tough taskmaster but she delivers her lectures with such a pretty smile, I hardly know I'm being fussed at."

"Oh, it's like that?" Rory asked with his own grin.

Santo held up his hand. "Oh, no. It's not like

that. We're existing in the same space at times. I see her when I get home each night and early each morning before I leave for work. Sometimes we talk on the phone, too. She's good at keeping me updated on how she's spending my money."

Maybe it *was* like that, he realized since he'd begun to enjoy those quick visits and her detailed updates. In fact, they had a meeting scheduled tonight at her apartment for a change.

"I'll think about what you've suggested," he told Rory. "I'm still trying to make amends for getting her confused with the nanny. Won't make that mistake again."

Two very different women and both of them trying to help him. He wondered what they'd thought, what they'd talked about once he'd left the house that first day. Still surprised at how attractive Davina Connell had turned out to be, he had to smile.

Rory picked up on that. "Well, you're looking more rested and it's good to see you smiling. I know Davina is not what you expected, but that could be a good thing."

Santo didn't comment. He wasn't ready to delve into his mixed feelings regarding his pretty contractor.

After Rory said a prayer with him and left

to go back to town, Santo sat and stared out at the river beyond the docks, wondering how he'd ever get over the horror of what had happened in his family.

The tall pines and old twisted oaks swayed in the spring breeze and the brownish-green water, filled with tannins and covered with a brackish sheen, moved in a steady flow to meet up with the bay. Everything moved, except him.

Once they were over the initial shock of Althea and Victor's betrayal and the scandal had died down, his parents had become even closer and surprisingly, more faithful to God. Rikki and Blain had gotten married just a few months after they'd confronted Althea in a cold, dank warehouse not far from here but they still had bad days, too. His brother, Victor, was sitting in prison, waiting for his sentence to be up so he could get back to gallivanting and spending more of the family funds. But Victor kept telling Santo he'd changed. He wanted to help out now.

Santo couldn't trust his brother on that yet. Victor would have to prove that he'd truly become a new man.

But Santo was here, unable to move. Paralyzed by a grief that he found both revolting and necessary. He grieved a woman he'd stopped loving long before she'd died and the guilt of that admission floored him and held him captive. His children deserved better and he needed to give everything he had to them. Not every material thing, but everything of himself.

How did he reconcile all the anger and bitterness inside his soul and go on with life even while he tried to raise his children shielded from the awful truth?

Santo sat there in the quiet of his office listening to the hum and flow coming from the warehouse. Shipments moved, employees went about their business and things got done.

He prayed for God to show him a way to make it all work together. A way to show his children that he loved them and would always protect them.

Preacher Rory had suggested he needed to be patient and he also needed to spend more time with his children. Thinking about Davina Connell and their meeting tonight, Santo decided it might time for him to make some changes, too.

Chapter Four

Davina eyed the I-Need-Chocolate-STAT cupcake she'd picked up at Marla's Marvelous Desserts and thought about how she was going to eat it while watching a movie she'd recorded two nights ago. One of the many nights she'd spent alone since she'd arrived here, which was perfectly fine with her. She loved to sketch ideas and jot down notes during her quiet time. She also loved to eat decadent chocolate desserts for dinner.

But her cell buzzed before she could make it across the space from the tiny den to the rectangular galley-style kitchen, where her prized cupcake set on the counter.

The caller ID lit up. Santo Alvanetti.

"Seriously," she said, glaring at the name and number. Now he was calling her at night?

Davina hit Accept on her cell and reminded

herself she was doing this to increase exposure for her fledgling construction company. And because she loved the old lake house Santo had purchased. Not quite Victorian and not quite Craftsman, the rambling white house with its deep porches and sturdy staircases begged for a new life and a good family. She'd be the one to give it new life and Santo could supply the family, but she planned to showcase this project big-time to increase awareness of the skills she and her employees could provide.

"Hello," she said into the phone, her eyes on that tempting cupcake with the marshmallow icing.

"Uh, hi. It's Santo. Did you still want to meet to go over the details of the renovations for the lake house?"

Davina groaned and glanced at the clock. "Uh…yes. I am so sorry. I forgot we agreed to meet tonight."

How could she have missed that important detail? Maybe because she'd been so busy all day, she'd agreed to this meeting in passing and didn't type it into her phone's calendar with a reminder.

She heard him inhale. "You weren't there when I got home, so we didn't verify."

Had he missed her?

Smiling, she said, "No, I left early to meet

Rikki at the lake house. We went over the whole house and I think we have a good plan. I just forgot about you coming here. I'm so sorry."

"It's okay, but I'd love to hear all about it," he said. "Mrs. Brownlee is available to stay with the children." He took a long breath. "And she made this amazing shrimp dish. I could bring some over."

This sounded almost like dinner, together. A date?

Davina didn't want to panic, but she felt that fluttering in her heart. It wasn't a good idea to get involved with a client. But then, she'd never had a client like this one. No wonder she'd pushed their meeting out of her head. She had to, to get him out of her head.

When she didn't answer, he rushed on. "I did come home early but I wanted to visit with the children and help them with their homework."

Davina had to admit that was sweet and impressive after the confusion and chaos she'd seen at his house a week ago. She was tired and she needed that cupcake. But she'd also agreed to meet him here so they could have some quiet time to discuss the lake house. And she really wanted to discuss that project in full.

"Do we need to reschedule?" he asked, the hesitation showing her a crack in his moody demeanor. At least he was coming around on being involved in the day-to-day decisions of renovating a house.

"Of course not," she said. "I'm here and I'm ready."

She ended the call and stared at her chocolate dinner. "You're going to have to wait," she decided, not wanting to gulp down her cupcake right before she met with him.

Grabbing a banana instead, she ate it and then fluffed her hair and put on some lip gloss and mascara.

She wouldn't change out of her leggings and tunic, however.

Davina had an early day tomorrow so she planned on staying casual and comfortable tonight. In spite of her rapidly beating heart.

She invited him in and plopped a huge chocolate cupcake on the counter. "I haven't had anything to eat since breakfast," Davina announced. "I'm starving and I'm going to eat this before I go to bed or someone is going to pay."

Santo actually chuckled and felt something like a jolt of heat moving through his heart. "And hello to you, too."

"Sorry." Her green eyes reminded him of a lush tropical forest. "I've had a long day and

I'm mortified that I completely forgot this meeting. That's not how I conduct business."

Santo should have insisted they cancel but he'd been looking forward to this all day long. But obviously, Davina had a lot more on her mind than spending a couple of hours with him. Which should have been okay, only he had to admit he felt a bit disappointed. But he'd get past that because she wasn't here to sit around with him. She had a lot of work to do yet.

Since he was here now, he carried on. "I've had some of the best shrimp fettuccine I've ever eaten for dinner," he said, handing her a warm plate covered with foil. "Miss Virginia is an amazing cook and she insisted I bring this over to you."

Davina's eyes lit up, causing yet another aftershock to charge through him. The woman was like an exotic chameleon, ever-changing. Then she said, "Are you going to feed me?"

He liked the way she asked that with a bit of a dare. "Yes, I am," he said. "Because I've had a long day, too, and…I want to make some changes in my life. That's one reason I wanted to talk to you alone tonight, without any interruptions from my wonderful children or their equally wonderful nanny."

She eyed him as if he'd turned into a sea

monster. "You mean changes such as being on time and being a little more organized? Or maybe being more available?"

"Ouch." Did he look like a total loser to her? "Yeah, those things and more." Watching as she sank onto a bar stool and dug into the shrimp dish with gusto, he said, "I guess I need to work on a lot of things." Then he glanced around the little beach-themed apartment. "At least Miss Virginia got the children to bed on time. She's a keeper."

"I'm sorry," she said between bites. "I shouldn't have implied you're not organized and involved with these projects. It's obvious you're doing the best you can. And yes, Mrs. Brownlee is a jewel."

Santo stayed across from her, the kitchen island separating them. He needed a buffer to remind him he'd hired her to help him, not so he could stand here and stare at her. "No, you have every right to be a little put out with me. First, I mistook you for the nanny and shoved one of my screaming children at you and then I left you and the real nanny standing in the middle of my den. And tonight, I didn't call until it was almost too late to have a business meeting. We could do this some other time."

"No, no," she said, waving her hand. "You're here now and I shouldn't judge you. I don't have children but I grew up in a big, crazy family. My mom, bless her, was always running behind. It drove me nuts but now I'm beginning to appreciate her efforts a whole lot more." She shrugged. "I have four siblings, so growing up, I watched several train wrecks and a whole lot of drama being played out. All my life, I only wanted some peace and quiet and to be my own person. I became a nomad of sorts, just to be by myself."

"So you don't get along with your family?"

"We get along," she explained. "Well, my older brother is also in construction and he resents me a tad but I ignore him. My younger brother is in the army so I don't get to see him much. But my sisters Tilly and Alana and I are close. We butt heads but we love each other."

She saw the darkness in his eyes, the searching glance.

"Do you ever get lonely?" he asked, the ache of his own loneliness echoing out around them.

"All the time," she admitted. "It's hard being a woman in construction but…I've always loved old houses and I want to fix up the one I grew up in one day. It's a beauty but it's falling apart. I want to do that for my parents if they'll allow me. We are a proud clan." She went on to tell him about her father's health and struggles. "I want to do what I can to keep them afloat since they've supported all of us through thick and thin."

Santo could see the remorse and the pride in her expression and in her eyes. Her amazing green eyes. "A big family, huh? That explains why you didn't complain when I threw Nate at you. You're probably used to that kind of messy morning."

She smiled at that. A pretty smile that seemed to make this tiny space shrink even more and go at least twenty degrees warmer. "Yes. I'm the middle one. Irish to the core, too. So you can only imagine fighting over the last slice of pizza or who got dibs on my mom's car on Saturday night."

"I'm thinking you won in both cases."

She laughed and dug into the shrimp again. Then she tore off a piece of the chunky French bread he'd included in the meal. "You'd better believe it. Being caught in the middle kept me out of the fray on either side. I got away with a lot."

Santo relaxed, his face muscles going slack, the constant ache in his neck loosing up the vise grip it had held on him for so long now. Glancing at her cupcake, he said the same thing he'd said about the Peaches-and-Cream cupcake they'd shared a few days ago. "I know where you bought that and I sure hope you're willing to share it."

"Let's go over my plans for the lake house and then we can fight over the cupcake. But I seem to remember I won last time."

"Can we negotiate?" he asked, realizing he just might be flirting with his house contractor. He'd forgotten how, but this felt dangerously close. Too close. It also felt refreshing and good. Too good. He'd made a vow to never open up his heart to a woman again. Santo had loved his wife but his love couldn't save their marriage or her. He'd been blinded by ambition and a need to please her, no matter the cost. Why would he want to risk that again? No, he'd go into this with his eyes wide open and his children as his first priority. Why would he put his children through any more trauma?

"Of course we can negotiate," Davina said, bringing him out of his anxious reevaluation. She opened her battered canvas tool bag and pulled out a notebook. "Everything is negotiable, right?"

"Right." But Santo decided this woman would be a tough adversary. And she probably always came out a winner. At least she'd keep him on his toes.

"Are you ready?" she asked, a bright glee in her eyes. "Let me show you what I have in mind to make your next home look like the showpiece it's supposed to be. Once I'm finished, you should be able to move your children into it knowing it's the best house it can be. I'll keep the historical integrity while updating the kitchens and baths, and adding charm to the living areas and bedrooms."

"You sound like those guys on that home network show that my mother used to watch all the time."

"I'm trying to sell you on the idea, so I practiced that speech."

"You're very convincing, so I'm ready," Santo replied, a new kind of excitement coursing through him. But he wasn't ready, really. He didn't have a clue about his old house or his new house or her or why he was so intent on moving. Maybe he wasn't trying to start a new life for his children. Maybe he was just running from the memories and the guilt associated with the showy, ostentatious house that had only brought him misery.

Chapter Five

Davina pulled out the sketches she'd made and then placed the original house plans she'd gotten from the former owner onto the counter. "Can you see?" she asked Santo, well aware of the hint of spice in his aftershave.

"I'll come around," he replied.

Both afraid of that and doing a happy dance in her head in spite of her fears, Davina reminded herself that she had to maintain a professional persona or she could very well mess up this project. So she took a calming breath and ran a hand over the plans and the photos she'd taken and printed out.

"This is an interesting house," she said, her excitement building with each word. "I can't wait to get started on it."

"And when will that be?" he asked over her

shoulder, the warmth radiating off of him like a welcome wind.

"In a week or so," she replied. "We've done a lot at the bay house since Mrs. Brownlee manages to get the kids out of the house while the construction crew is there."

"Yes, they've been going over to my parents' place a lot," he said. "My parents are on a cruise right now, but the kids love it there anyway. And our housekeeper still lives here, so she's a help with them, too."

Rikki had told Davina that their parents lived in a big house on the bay not far from Santo's house. The Alvanetti compound was off the road and secluded and had a large horse stable and pasture attached. A perfect place for kids to play. A place that used to have armed guards, according to the gossip she picked up on here and there.

"Well, I'm glad they have somewhere to hang out after school," she said. "Anyway, we're almost done with the floors and the walls have been painted and freshened and the furniture edited down a bit. Rikki and I picked out some lovely rugs and vases from your store earlier this week."

"You were in the store?" he asked, surprise in his dark eyes. "You should have come back to the warehouse and office. I would have given you a tour."

"We were in a hurry," she said. "And I didn't want to bother you."

No need to visit the man at work unless she had something really important to discuss with him. Which could happen one day since she'd have a million decisions to make during renovations.

"That can only mean my sister went over budget on whatever she bought, even with the family discount."

"*Because* of the family discount," Davina replied with a grin. "But the bay house is coming along. What do you think about it so far?"

He studied the plans in front of them and then looked up at her with admiration. "You've done an amazing job. I couldn't see it before but you've brought out the integrity of the place. Now I know what a mid-century modern is supposed to look like, at least."

Davina wanted to hug him for complimenting her work. But even more wonderful, he understood what she'd try to accomplish with his swank waterfront property. The big house still had its industrial planes and angles but she'd added color and fire and brightness that brought the outside in and merged the house with the bluffs and the bay beyond.

"I'm glad you're pleased," she said. "It should be ready for you to list soon." She poured him a glass of water and then refilled her glass. Then she named the estimated selling price.

"Wow, that much?"

She laughed at the shock on his face. "Yes, that much. I did a good job."

"I think you did." He tapped a finger on the plans. "On to the new house. What do you want to do there?"

She laughed and tugged at her haphazard bun. "So much. A complete overhaul." When she looked up, he was staring at her with a look akin to awe and longing.

"Santo? Are you okay?"

He nodded. "Uh...yes." His gaze moved over her face and then settled on her hair. "I've just never known a contractor with such beautiful hair."

A hot blush moved down Davina's neck. Great. Now she'd get the blotchies, as her sister Tilly always called them. A flush that only showed off her freckles. Maybe he wouldn't notice.

He kept staring at her.

"Santo, the house?"

"Oh, yes, the house," he said with a wry smile. "I need to focus on the house."

Frantic now, she searched her notes. What

was happening to her, anyway? She never acted like a ninny with clients. But then she'd never had a client who'd commented on her hair in such an intimate way. The room grew warm, the air stifling.

"It's a lovely house," she said, regaining her footing while she didn't make eye contact. "Only one owner for the last fifty years or so and with a big family that's scattered now. He's in an assisted living home up in Milton."

She took a breath and stared at the house plan. "I went and visited with Mr. Floyd so I could get a feel for the place. He told me all about his wife, Katie, and their four boys. Kind of reminded me of my family back in Louisiana. They lovingly took care of the home but no one has lived in it for a couple of years and it needs some updates. The kitchen is quaint but outdated and, of course, the bathrooms need major overhauls."

He laughed and nodded, his smile radiating even more heat. "Of course."

Davina had to swallow. Grabbing her water, she gulped it too fast and started coughing.

"Are you okay?" Santo asked, those all-seeing eyes moving over her again.

"Yes." She hacked another round and prayed the blotchies were gone by now. "Just…not very ladylike."

He smiled and pointed to her notes. "So I think I'm beginning to see how you operate. You redo the current house to sell and you redo the new house before anyone can move in. You've got quite a racket going here, don't you?"

Seeing the mirth in his eyes, Davina nodded. "Of course. I make money on both ends of the deal. My mama raised me right."

"Smart." He leaned close and she became transported to some exotic spot where herbs and spices were rich and sweet and enticing. The man smelled like something unique and fresh and forbidden. An outdoor market, a quiet alfresco café, a moonlit night in some faraway place.

Get over it, Davina.

"So not only are you smart but you're also pretty and you can outwork any man I've ever met. You're amazing."

"You haven't seen the final bill yet," she quipped, only because she was about to hyperventilate. "Anyway, so we have the first floor. We'll start with sprucing up the entire outside, of course. Fresh white paint and new shutters in keeping with all of the designs around the lake."

"Yes, we need to keep up with appearances," he said.

"Historical features," she corrected. "You know Lake Street is a prestigious and unique oval road that runs all along the lake."

"Yes, I know that. That's why I decided to buy there. The kids love it when we go to Alec Caldwell's house."

"Oh, the big Victorian with the turret on top. I love that house. A perfect example of preserving the historical features while bringing a home into this century. Just gorgeous."

"My sister loves it, too."

"Alec and Marla are so nice," Davina said, glad to be on a safe subject. "And I've gained five pounds because I seem to go by her café just about every day."

Santo eyed the chocolate cupcake. "Yes, you do travel with one of those hidden in your big bag at all times, right?"

"Right."

"Let's get on with this so I can sample your treat."

His gaze wasn't on that cupcake.

He was staring at her lips.

Davina swallowed again but refrained from grabbing her water. "So we have the downstairs master with a lovely sitting area. I know you wanted some office space—"

"You do?"

He looked so surprised, she laughed. "Yes,

because your sister told me. Thank goodness she knows what you'd like to happen with this house."

"I haven't talked to her in a while."

"Well, then, she's making decisions for you. Good ones, though."

Santo ran a hand through his hair and tugged at it as if he wanted to pull it all out by the roots. "I need to become more involved in this, don't I?"

Davina motioned to the sofa. "Let's talk."

He sat down with her and gave her a helpless glance. "My wife always took care of any repairs or updates on our house. But I didn't always agree with her taste."

Having witnessed Rikki's gaudy taste, Davina could agree with that.

"If you don't get involved, you can't complain," she said. "Why don't you tell me what you want in a new home, Santo?"

He leaned forward and templed his fingers over his knees. "Everyone keeps asking me that," he said. "They ask me why I'm leaving such a stunning house and that amazing view."

"And what do you tell them? Or what is it you're not telling them?"

He kept staring at his hands. "I tell them I'm ready for a change, that the kids need something different and more kid-friendly."

"That's all true," Davina replied. "But I need to know more. I need to know your heart. Because when I renovate a home for someone new to move into, I want to show that family's heart in everything I do. I don't know your heart."

"You don't want to know my heart," he said, getting up, his mood dark now. "And me coming here was a bad idea. Just remodel the place and make it livable, Davina. That's what I'm paying you for."

Davina couldn't give up in spite of the glaring warning in his eyes. "What else are you willing to pay for?"

"What does that mean?"

"I'm worried that you're moving for all the wrong reasons."

"Do you want me to find another contractor?"

"No," she said, her determination giving her the courage to face him. "I want this job. I need this job. But I also want to understand you… so I can make you a home that you'll appreciate and be happy in."

"I don't know if I'll ever be completely happy again," he said, his hands on his hips, his eyes full of a raging torment. "But…I want my children to be happy. I want them to have a tree house and swings and I want them to go fishing on the pier by the lake. I want to take long walks with them and read to them and hold them when they're afraid. I want to stop their nightmares and show them that we're going to be all right."

He halted, his eyes filling with dread and apprehension. "I don't like talking about this. Just do what you need to do, and leave me out of the details."

He turned to go.

But she moved in front of him. "I'm sorry. I shouldn't have pushed. But, Santo, what you just told me gives me a whole different perspective."

"I'm sure it does," he said, anger coloring the words. "Now you feel pity for me and my poor children, right?"

"No. Not pity. I admire you for what you're trying to do. Why don't you cut yourself some slack and become part of the process. There's healing in renovating things, especially houses. They can tell a story."

"And what does my current home tell you?"

"That you're lonely and full of guilt."

He stood at the door, his head turned toward the wide window that showcased the old live oaks and palm trees and the lake beyond. "I came here thinking I was ready to dive in and help you, put in some physical labor. But I don't think I can do this, Davina. All I know is my own work and it consumes me because I had to bring my family out of a disaster. I stay busy and I try to get home and spend time with my children. I try to sleep."

"But you don't sleep, do you?"

He shook his head and stayed silent.

"You've been through something horrific and traumatic," she said. "I don't expect you to share all the details with me."

Whirling, he dropped his arms to his sides. "But you've heard the details. It made the national news. The whole world knows what happened to my family, to my children. To my wife and me. No wonder my parents decided to leave the country."

Then Davina saw it in his eyes. The shame, the despair, the regret, the guilt. "It wasn't your fault."

He shook his head. "Doesn't matter. I'm the one who's still here. I'm the one who has to protect my children and show them that we have to get on with our lives."

"And you're doing that," she said, moving closer to him. "This house will be sunny and bright and full of joy. I'll see to that. But Santo, you'll have to do your part, too."

He gave her a twisted smirk. "And how do I do that? I've been dealing with this for over a year now. The first few months, I was too numb to feel anything. But my children needed me so I had to find a way to keep moving. So what part do I play now? What can I do to make this right again? How can I do anything more?"

"By forgiving your wife," she replied. "And yourself."

"Stop it, please," he replied on a quiet tone. "I didn't hire you to be my spiritual counselor. Your work is good, Davina. Let's leave it at that."

"Okay. I'm sorry I overstepped," she said, her heart breaking for this man. "I've never been through anything like what you've had to deal with. I came from a loving, happy, chaotic family but we didn't have a lot of money. So I'm driven to prove myself and sometimes in my zest to make a house perfect, I ask too many personal questions. It won't happen again."

Lifting his head, he almost spoke but stopped himself. After a brief silence that told her exactly how he felt, he said, "I'll check in with you again soon."

"Okay. Thank you for the dinner." She glanced at the cupcake they'd never shared, her stomach roiling in protest, her nerves tangled tighter than electrical cords. "I'll make sure you get the official reports on both houses."

"I appreciate that," he said.

And then he turned and walked out the door.

Davina watched him get into his car and zoom away.

And then she sank down on the couch and started praying.

Dear Lord, help this man to heal. Watch over him and his precious children. And please guide me in renovating this home for them.

Because she knew in her heart that it would take a lot more than hammers and nails to mend this broken family.

Chapter Six

Davina couldn't get the conversation she'd had with Santo last night out of her mind. Not that she hadn't stayed busy. She'd finished up the last details on the bay house today and planned to spend most of the afternoon over at the fixer-upper lake house. Since Santo had told her to do what she needed to get the place in order, she had the go-ahead, such as it was. But she'd really hoped he'd change his mind and decide to get more involved in this project. He needed to see the skeleton of the house, test its bones, learn its structure and explore every nook and cranny because that was exactly what his children would do.

How could anyone not want to do that with a house?

Maybe Santo wasn't wired like her. Tilly

and Alana teased her about loving houses more than she loved wanting a home of her own.

Her sisters had a point. Houses were easy to love, easy to shape and mold and change. People, not so much. Davina wasn't good at building relationships, probably because she'd always been right smack in the middle of her family's sometimes tempestuous relationships with each other. But no matter now. Santo had made it clear he wasn't good at that either. Or so he thought.

Since Davina didn't want that lovely old home to become cold and rigid like the bay house, she'd keep her mind centered on making it spectacular again. Glad she was finished here, she did like how the modern beauty was coming along nicely. But working around the children had been a challenge.

Thinking about Santo's beautiful children made her smile in spite of the intensity of their words last night. She'd miss these kids once she was done completely. She'd miss this community, too.

"I think I'll be a carpenter like you when I grow up," nine-year-old Lucia announced this morning when Davina walked through the door. "It's a lot of fun. I like hammering things the way you do. And you're always laughing and smiling."

The dark-haired beauty with eyes so like her father's hadn't witnessed Davina screaming at plumbers or discussing with the tile man why the counters didn't fit. That was because when the children were around, Davina tried to make the whole reconstruction fun and interesting as long as they stayed clear of any danger. She'd even found each of them bright yellow hard hats to wear. Which earned her points with the kids and Mrs. Brownlee and brought a scowl from their dad.

She wouldn't tell him she'd also let them hammer some nails into old boards, with both Mrs. Brownlee and herself supervising. Her parents had been protective but also lenient when letting their children explore and learn things. She hoped if she ever had any children, she'd be the same. But watching Santo's children run around this treacherously beautiful house had brought out all of the maternal instincts she didn't even know she had.

"This is a fun job," she told Lucia now with a big grin. "You would be very good at it since you've had practice bossing your brother and sister around. And taking care of them," she added, because Lucia did help with her younger siblings.

"I have to be the boss," Lucia replied with a stern expression, her eyes growing even bigger. "I'm the oldest and we don't have a mom anymore." Then she'd lowered her voice. "She went to heaven."

Davina squatted and took Lucia's hand, wishing she hadn't teased so much. "I know and I'm so sorry about that. You're a great big sister. And your daddy is so proud of you."

"He acts mad all the time."

Davina could vouch for that. Her heart tumbled over itself, seeing the serious concern in Lucia's eyes. What must this child think about the horrible thing that had happened in her life?

Putting on her best reassuring face, Davina shook her head. "No, no, he's just got so much to take care of. He works hard so he can provide for all of you. He loves you."

"He tells us that," Lucia said in a matter-of-fact voice. "Sometimes I wish he'd just stay home with us. Saturday is supposed to be fun day and this Saturday, there's a festival on the lake but he won't remember. Mommy used to say that Daddy only remembered work and nothing else. But I don't think he forgets on purpose. I wish he'd go with us, though."

Before Davina could respond to the little anxious girl, her sister, Adriana, ran by and screamed, "Nate's hiding. And he's not wearing his hard hat."

After that, a game of cat and mouse had

ensued and soon, Davina and Mrs. Brownlee were both highly involved. They'd found the little boy in the corner of the master bedroom, hiding behind a big rocking chair that Davina had just placed by the locked doors out onto a cedar terrace.

"I like this chair," Nate said, a finger to his mouth. "Can you rock me?"

Davina looked at Mrs. Brownlee and nodded. "I certainly can." So while Virginia took the girls to the kitchen for a snack, Davina rocked Nate to sleep, her mind going back and forth with the cadence of the heavy wood hitting the plush carpet.

A girl could get used to that kind of cadence.

The little boy had lifted his head and smiled at her. "Da-danina."

"Davina," she'd said, grinning down at him.

Nate shook his head. "Danina." Then he snuggled closer, burrowing into her arms. And into her heart.

As he drifted off, Davina had whispered close, "Dani. I'm Dani."

A soft giggle had erupted against her heartbeat.

The sweetness of that moment had stayed with her all day. Now she was finished. The crew would come back and clean things up and do a run-through and then, she'd do a final walk-through with Santo and see if they'd missed anything. Not that he would notice or care.

She'd purposely been late this morning. Yes, she was avoiding him. It was for the best. The man was in a world of hurt and she'd pushed him too far, too soon, last night.

"Mind your own business," her mother always told her children. They never did, of course. Nor did Ma. Ma was a caring, loving soul who could spot a hurting heart from a mile away, human or animal. She'd be over the moon with these three Alvanetti children and she'd immediately insist they needed a big dog to follow them around.

"Are you really all done?" Mrs. Brownlee asked through a sigh, her hands held together over the apron that stated Free Hugs with Each Cookie.

"I am," Davina said. "And in record time. This job would normally take at least a month but when you have an unlimited budget, you can get things done pretty quickly. Three weeks for a general overhaul is my personal best now."

"Yes, you did seem to hurry this into overdrive," her new friend pointed out, sparkly red earrings warring with her auburn curls. "I take it you and Santo don't always see eye to eye."

"He's tough to read," Davina replied, glad to be able to have a confidante. "Some walls can't be torn down because there's no support beam."

"He needs to find his faith again," Mrs. Brownlee said. "And no, you can't do that for the poor man." She shrugged and stared out at the water. "We each have to walk our own faith path and it can be fraught with detours."

Davina gathered her things to leave, wondering about Virginia's detours. "I'll arrange the walk-through after the workers have cleaned up. I'll get together with Santo on that and then we can list the house."

"I can keep the children occupied for you."

"Thank you," Davina said. "I guess they don't need to see the final version of the house they're leaving."

Mrs. Brownlee glanced at the glistening bay beyond the small bluff. "They're already excited about moving to the lake." She pointed outside. "That water down there is out of reach for them, but the lake has always been the center of this town. It will do them good to fish in the shallows and ride their bikes along the trails. They're isolated here in this cold tower.

There, they'll meet friends and have neighbors all around."

"I hope so," Davina said, turning to head for the door before Virginia picked up on how much she'd miss the children. She'd just put her hand on it when it flew open and Santo stood there, blocking the light. Stepping back before she got banged, Davina held on to the tidal wave of feelings surging around her.

"You're home early," Mrs. Brownlee said, pointing out the obvious.

"Am I?" he asked, his eyes on Davina. "Where are you going?"

"To the lake house to meet with Rikki," she replied. "I'm done here."

"So soon?" He glanced at his watch.

"I've been telling you for days that I would be finished by the end of the week." She shrugged. "It's the end of the week."

He rubbed his head as if to get answers. "What about the final...look?"

Davina shot Virginia a glance and looked back at him. "The workers have to clean out any debris and tools and then we can do that later. Maybe Monday, after you're done with work?"

"How about now?"

Davina waffled between telling him yes or no.

"Nate's asleep," Mrs. Brownlee said. "And the girls are in the game room watching an animated movie."

Santo paced a foot or so. "So it's not a good time?"

"It would be better if we do that on Monday," Davina said, steeling herself for his reaction.

A curt nod. "Okay, then I'll walk you to your car."

Did he want to talk to her?

"All right." She moved to leave.

"Daddy!"

Lucia rushed up to him and Santo took her into his arms. Adriana followed and soon both girls were giggling into Santo's ears.

He looked at Davina, a smile cresting on his face. "You two are certainly in a good mood."

Lucia bobbed her head, her dark curls whirling around her face and shoulders like inky swatches of silk. "That's 'cause we have the best idea ever."

"Oh? And what's that?" Santo asked, still smiling even if his eyes had gone dark again.

"The Millbrook Lake Art Festival," Lucia said through another giggle. "It's tomorrow, Daddy. And we want to go. With you and Miss Davina."

Santo's grin went slack.

Davina's heart went bump.

And Virginia Brownlee chuckled and watched the whole scene with a little too much mirth in her eyes.

"I'll explain to her later," Santo said once he'd told Lucia he'd have to consider her request.

"I'll probably be at the festival anyway," Davina said. "Vanessa told me about it. Lots of local art and good fresh seafood and the weather's supposed to be nice." She hesitated and then went on. "I could take the kids."

Surprised, Santo shook his head. "Oh, no. You don't know what you're offering. They'd all take off in three different directions and you'd spend the whole day rounding them back up."

"I can handle them," she said, her tone firm. "Lucia is set on going and…she mentioned you'd probably forget."

Wow, straight to the heart. His pretty contractor could sling more than a hammer. "She said that to you?"

"Yes. But I'm sure Virginia would love to go, too. Together, we should be able to keep your children corralled."

"You seem a bit aggravated," he pointed out.

"You seem a bit surprised," she retorted.

"I'm sorry," he finally said. "I was rude to you last night and I didn't mean to be. I'd still like to be more involved in the new house, if you still want me to be."

"It's not what I want," Davina said, thinking right now she wanted a lot of things. "It's what you need to do. Most people who buy a house want to check it out and study it and walk through it several times. You have an amazing yard and one of the best views of the lake. Or do you even remember those things?"

He had to stop and think. "Rikki was with me during the final walk-through and she did the looking. I had to get back to a meeting."

Davina's pained expression told him she wasn't impressed with him. "So you don't know anything about the house you bought?"

He stared up the street, watching as a row of palm trees danced in the wind. "No, I guess I don't. I looked at it once by myself and told Rikki to handle the details. I didn't really give it my full attention the day we closed."

"Then I'll handle my details with your sister," Davina said. "I have to go. I'm supposed to meet her there anyway."

"I could come along," he said, wishing he'd been better prepared for this woman.

"That is up to you, of course."

But he saw the flare of hope in her expressive eyes.

"You go ahead and after I visit with the kids awhile, I'll meet you there."

"Right." She didn't sound sure.

But then, neither was he.

Chapter Seven

"Your brother should be here to help with these decisions," Davina told Rikki once she arrived at the lake house. Still reeling from his moods and his recent abrupt change of heart, she added, "This place needs a major overhaul but I want to talk to him and show him what I plan before I get started. He said he'd be here later but I'm not going to count on that."

"Oh, no," Rikki said. "Did he upset you again?"

"How do you know he's ever upset me?" Davina asked, appalled that it showed.

"Because my brother makes everyone mad sooner or later. He has that knack. It took Blain many months to get used to Santo and his quick mood swings."

"Months?" Davina didn't have months to work out the kinks in her relationship with the man footing the bills. "I just want him to care about this for a few days at least." She moved through the empty house, the echo of her frustrations following her. "Maybe two or three months on this one, actually. I want to take my time and give this graceful old lady a proper makeover."

Rikki's dark eyes, so like her brother's, filled with an apologetic darkness. "Santo is always busy. He trusts us to do what we have to do so it'll be his fault if he doesn't like the end result. But honestly, I don't think he'll care. He just wants to get his children out of the bay house. I think the memories finally got to him. Instead of going away, they starting crowding around him. And I know Lucia has had some nightmares and some of her friends have made cruel comments about her mother. The children have talked to counselors but what happened has been hard on my family." She shook her head. "Blain and I talk about it still. He had to kill Althea, but…it's just been so hard on all of us."

"I'm sorry," Davina said, her aggravation with Santo overshadowing the fact that Rikki had been targeted and almost murdered by her own sister-in-law. "I'm so sorry for you and Blain. And Santo, too. I don't mean to sound insensitive. I get so caught up in the job I forget everything else. You went through this, along with your whole family. I mean, you could have been killed. But you seem to be handling it a lot better than Santo."

Rikki's grim expression softened. "If I didn't have Blain, I'd have nightmares all the time, too. I lost my best friend and my ex-boyfriend. Althea killed both of them and my brother, Victor, had to go to prison. He was so involved with her he didn't see until it was too late that she'd gone off the deep end. None of us did."

She stopped and took a breath. "I think that's the main thing eating at Santo. That he didn't know his own wife and that his children could have been in real danger. He and Althea had an intense relationship from the beginning but it burned out in a very bad way. She only wanted the money and what she thought he could give her. He tried so hard to please her, but Althea was beyond pleasing. She always wanted more."

Davina thought about Santo and his moods. "It must be horrible, having to carry that burden. Maybe I need to stop pushing him on this and just get the work done."

"No, he needs someone besides family to help him see past his grief," Rikki replied, her expression full of encouragement. "And I think you might be the perfect person for that."

"I met him barreling through the door as I

was leaving to come here," Davina said. "Intense does not even describe the man." She hesitated and then said, "He told me a little bit about what he's been through. He's a proud man, Rikki. But he loves those children so much."

"Yes, anyone can see that," Rikki said. "He's trying to spend more time with them."

"Well, he had his hands full with your adorable nieces this afternoon." She made notes on the hardwood floors. A good buffing could bring some new luster to them. "I'll try to be gentle with him but I so want him to help with this, for his own sake."

Rikki's expression changed to worry. "He can't seem to keep a good nanny but Virginia is hanging in there. I worked hard finding someone I thought could tough it out. She's perfect. A widow but still young at heart. Of course, it's only been three weeks." She laughed. "That's a long run for Santo and his kids."

"I think that problem's been solved," Davina replied. She went on to tell Rikki about Virginia's many outstanding qualities. "She takes his gruffness right in stride."

"He's always had an edge about him," Rikki replied, her long dark ponytail falling across one shoulder while she measured the old Formica countertops. "Brooding and moody. That describes Santo. Now Victor on the other hand—all fun and games and...currently sitting in prison for five years."

Wishing she hadn't said anything, Davina tried again. "Don't worry. I can handle Santo. I'll do what I need to do and send him the bill. But I want you to be my witness and help me go over some of my concerns here. The bay house is done and it looks a lot better. I think it will go quickly, so I need to get kicking on this one."

"I'll help where I can," Rikki replied. "And Santo will get my bill, too."

"How's your house coming?" Davina asked, to change the subject. Rikki and her husband, Blain Kent, a detective with the Millbrook police, had bought a bungalow not far from here. But it had already been updated by the previous owners so Rikki was adding some finishing touches to make it more personal. The one-level house was cozy and colorful and filled with a coastal cottage decor.

"It's great," she said. "I'm going through each room at a time and having fun doing it. I can't wait to shop for art and knickknacks at the festival tomorrow."

"The kids want to come to that festival," Davina said. "I'm not so sure your brother will bring them." She didn't add the part about being invited to come along with them. Rikki didn't need to hear that. No one needed to hear that.

Rikki took a few photos of the beadboard walls in the big, rambling kitchen. Davina planned to clean up the white subway tiles along the backsplash and maybe salvage the black-and-white-tiled floors, too. With sturdy rugs scattered here and there.

"Santo doesn't like crowds," Rikki said. "He's really more of an introvert."

"I can tell," Davina replied, jotting notes and measuring yet again to get a feel for fresh new white cabinets and shimmering marble countertops. The breakfast room was square and sunny, with a big paned window that showed off the long back porch and the fenced-in yard. Good place for the kids to play away from the water across the narrow Lake Street in front of the house.

But the lake side was even better. A big, deep porch that begged for a light blue ceiling in keeping with the Southern tradition of fooling insects into thinking the ceiling was part of the sky, and fresh gray planked floors to hide dirt and feel cool on bare feet. She'd update the sturdy columns and refurbish the wide front door with the exquisite stained glass panels. Those would stay. The porch needed red geraniums and flowing ferns, rocking chairs and settees, a big swing for the children.

The house had an unobstructed view of the center of the big lake. Even now, she could see a red-and-white sailboat gliding along on the silent wind. The old, moss-covered oaks and deeply rooted camellia bushes and azaleas only added to the charm. The smell of jasmine and magnolias lingered throughout the rooms since she and Rikki had opened the doors wide to bring in the fresh air.

"I love this house. I want your brother to love it, too."

Davina could see it all. And for the first time in her career, she wanted to stick around to see beyond the finished project. She wanted this to work, to be a safe haven for Santo and his children.

An image of herself inserted in that picture caused her to inhale a breath. She'd prayed for this little family but now her heart had rearranged itself for them. She had to make this right. With the Lord's guidance, she knew she could create a safe haven in this old house.

"Are you okay?" Rikki asked from the massive dining room.

"Yes, just so many ideas."

"You'll make this place a showcase," Rikki

called. "I can't wait to see what you do with it. I'm excited about helping you decorate it."

"Because you know I'm going to do what's right and because you'll know how to fill in the blanks for me," Davina said as they met in the wide central hallway. "I'm going to make this house shine so Santo can bring his children into a sunny, bright, happy home. A real home."

"That's exactly why I hired you," Rikki said. "You're the best at what you do and I need someone who can get around Santo and his issues to make this work. He'd never listen to me and he'd try to force me to keep the cost down. Those children need a safe, calm environment that's comfortable and childproof. Not some showplace that looks like it needs to be in a magazine. They need a home. A real home. You can give them that, Davina."

"I'd like to hear how she plans on doing that."

They both turned to the open French doors leading to the back porch and found Santo standing there in a button-up shirt and jeans, his hands stuffed into his pants pockets, and his eyes on Davina.

"We were just discussing how I'm going to do that," Davina said, determined to be strong and stand up to his black moods.

"Show me your plans," he said. "I want to hear about all of it."

Rikki gave Davina a steady stare, her dark eyes full of surprise and awareness. "Well, okay then."

Davina couldn't speak, had barely squeaked out a quick response at seeing him there. Unusual but then, Santo made her whole system short-circuit.

"You do still want me involved, don't you?" he asked, giving her a daring once-over.

"Of course." Only now, she wasn't so sure that was a good idea after all.

The way the man was looking at her had nothing to do with renovating a house. But it had everything to do with destroying her heart.

Santo didn't know what had come over him. "I…uh…wanted to see this house again. To make sure I made the right decision."

Rikki glanced at her watch. "I only have a few minutes before I meet Blain for dinner. I'm going upstairs to take pictures and stare at blank walls."

His sister took off so fast her sneakers barely hit the stairs as she scurried up and away.

Santo kept his gaze on Davina and hoped she was still speaking to him. "Can you show me the house?"

"Do you really want to do this?" she asked, her green eyes wild with distrust and something he didn't want to recognize. Compassion? Pity? Understanding? She must have a war going on inside that pretty head, and if so, he was pretty sure he'd cast himself as the enemy she was trying to fight.

He walked up the empty hallway, the old planks croaking and groaning against the weight of his steps. "Yes. I want you to guide me through this renovation."

"No, I mean do you really want to leave the bay house?"

"Of course I do," he said. But even while he said the words, his heart lurched at the thought of changing his life so completely. He owed Davina the truth on that, at least. Closing his eyes for a second, he took a long breath. "This is going to be hard. Uprooting my children could cause them to go off on a tailspin again. They need stability and security."

"They'll find it here," she said. "Once Rikki and I are finished, this place will look like a big playhouse."

"They need a home, not a playhouse."

Discouragement took the bright glow out of her eyes. "What do you want me to do, Santo? You say one thing, but then I feel as if you mean something else entirely. I don't need mixed signals. I need decisiveness and consistency."

The woman didn't back down. He'd give her that. And she was right.

"I'm sorry. I shouldn't have said that. I'm a wreck about this move. Months ago when I decided to do this, it felt like it was for the best. I'd lost yet another nanny and the kids were acting out. I thought it was just because of the hectic Christmas break, but it was because they missed having Christmas with their mother. She died right before Christmas the year before last. So after yet another sad holiday, I started early in the year looking for something different. It became an obsession and then I saw a for-sale sign on this place and…I bought it after one walk-through."

Moving another step closer, he looked into Davina's eyes. "I don't normally act so impulsively but something grabbed at me that day because Lucia had been harassed at school. I talked with her teachers and her counselors and we addressed the problem, but I needed to do something more. I had this need to find a fresh start. A need to see my children in a big backyard with a secure fence. The water across the street, nearby instead of right there and down below a dangerous bluff. The porches and the beautiful wide staircase made me think of how happy my children could be here. This place seemed like what I'd been longing for. Can you understand what I'm saying?"

Davina's whole expression changed, softened, mellowed. Holding his gaze, she moved close. No islands or counters stood between them here in the big, wide heart of this house. They were in open territory. The house stilled, almost as if a sigh had moved through the walls. Rikki's sneakered feet walking around upstairs didn't even touch them here in this cocoon.

"I understand," she said. "More than you will ever know. It's a lovely house, Santo. I can picture you and your children here. This house needs a good family. Houses, just like humans, tend to wither up and fade away if they aren't cared for and lived in."

Santo swallowed the pain that cut through his vocal cords like a whipping anchor rope. "I felt like that, yes. As if I was slowly fading away, dying inside. This house changed all of that."

"And now?"

"And now, I'm afraid I made a big mistake. I walk around the bay house and…I hurt all over again. I'm taking my children from the only home they've ever known. I remember good times there. Althea was very convincing. She pretended to care. She tried to be a good mother but she wanted more than any of us were willing to give." Putting two fingers to his forehead, he rubbed the spot that pounded like a storm surge. "What if my children aren't happy here either?"

Davina touched a hand to his arm. "Santo, your children will be happy with *you*, no matter where you are. Show them all the love you tried to show their mother. Show them how to be strong and how to recover from this. Help me build you a new home with new memories and let them be involved in this project so they feel ownership, too."

Santo's heart beat too fast. He'd never been scared of anything or anyone in his life but he'd had a good life, a pampered, privileged, protected life up until that fatal day when Althea had been killed. Now, he couldn't breathe. And he prayed he wouldn't humiliate himself and have a panic attack in front of Davina.

As if sensing his need to turn and leave, Davina took his hand in hers. Her hand was strong and soft, calloused but gentle, warm and firm and sure, her fingers tightening against his in what felt like a varnish of protection.

"I'll be right here," she said. "But I need you to be here with me. I think that once we get going on this, you'll be able to work through some of this anxiety and concern. You can take ownership, a real ownership of your new home."

"And will this help me work through my nightmares?" he asked, holding his emotions in a tightly coiled entanglement.

"I believe so," she said, her gaze caught in his, her green eyes giving him the peace of a cool summer forest.

When they heard Rikki coming down the wooden stairs, their gazes slammed together and then they broke apart, both physically and emotionally. But Santo still felt the warmth from Davina's touch.

Now his heart pulsed a new kind of beat. One that had a lifeline.

"What's up?" his sister asked, suspicion and surprise in the question.

"I'm going to help," he said. "Starting next week."

"Okay," Rikki replied, clearly sensing the static that crackled through the empty room. "I'm glad you two worked that out."

Santo nodded and finally smiled, a great rush of relief pouring over him. "Because tomorrow we have plans."

"What kind of plans?" Rikki asked while Davina kept watching him.

"The kids and I will be attending the Millbrook Lake Art Festival. And I have strict orders to bring Davina with us."

He hadn't planned on blurting that out. He hadn't planned on including the pretty contractor in their outing. But now, he wanted her with him. He needed the comfort she seemed to bring to his tattered soul.

"Are you interested?" he asked, waiting.

"I…uh…" She glanced from him to Rikki.

Rikki crossed her arms and gave Davina a knowing nod followed by a look of awe aimed toward him.

"I'd love to attend the festival with you and your children," Davina said. "Sounds like it'll be a good day."

Santo nodded and then whirled around. "Okay, so now I can see my house."

Chapter Eight

Davina wasn't sure where to begin. She wasn't even sure what had just happened between them. Rikki made a few suggestions and left, moving faster than Davina had ever seen before.

She'd talk to Rikki later. Right now, she intended to give Santo her best pitch on how to renovate and restore this rambling house.

"Let's start with the kitchen," she said. Then she went on to explain how she'd tear out the old walnut cabinets and put in fresh white wood. "With white marble countertops but with curved edges. More childproof."

"Do you see how the kitchen and breakfast room flow right into the big living room?" she asked, already creating a new space in her head. "I want to knock out this wall between the kitchen and the living area to open up this space. So when Virginia is in the kitchen, she can easily see the kids in the living area. I plan to build them a play area upstairs but for here, they'll have a corner nook for reading and homework, complete with their own television—for approved movies and shows."

She lifted her hand to indicate the corner by the back porch that would be perfect for their study nook. "And the fireplace will be cleaned and updated with new tiles and maybe I can find some repurposed wood to update the mantel."

"Wood can be repurposed?" he asked, his dark eyes shiny with interest.

"Anything can be repurposed," she said, nodding. "I know a place over in Alabama that specializes in old wood. Doors, window frame, boarding from walls. You'd be amazed at what people throw out or give away."

"I am amazed," he said, his tone quiet. "I have a lot to learn."

"You could add wood to your business," she suggested. "Have a spot in your warehouse where people can come and shop for exotic or hard-to-find wood products and pieces."

He laughed at that. "Wow, slow down. Let's get the house finished before you take over my business."

Davina reeled in her enthusiasm. "Well,

Rikki tells me you're expanding. You have the store now for retail, right?"

"Yes." He walked around the big rectangular kitchen and leaned forward to glance out the big, tall windows. "Alvanetti Imports is now selling retail straight from the warehouse. So far, we're doing pretty well. We sell to a lot of the condo developers and to people building or renovating private homes."

"So you could use some beautiful wood and wood products?"

"Stop it," he said, wagging a finger at her. "You're a bad influence."

"I've never heard that one before," she admitted. "I was always the good daughter."

"Tell me about your family," he said as they moved around the living room and then on to the formal dining room.

"Not much to tell. My parents are hard-working and simple. I have two sisters and two brothers—an older one and younger one of each. I'm the middle child. My mother was a teacher but she's retired now. My father owned and sold his own construction company but he's still a contractor. I got my love of building things from him. My older brother works with Da and my younger other one is in the army. My younger sister, Tilly, and I are very close, but my other sister, Alana, is single and she lives in New Orleans. We don't see her much because she's mad at the world these days because the man she's loved since high school ran off with another woman right before their wedding."

"You and I have that in common," Santo said. "Big families with lots of issues."

"I couldn't get away fast enough," she admitted.

She took him into the big master bedroom down a short hallway from the living area. "Now in here, you have your room and bath with a great view on either side—the yard and the lake." She pointed to the bay window across from the wall where she and Rikki had agreed the bed should go. "You needed dedicated space for your home office. I think this could be it. A desk in front of those windows and a nice view of the porch and the yard beyond. And you have a French door right off to the side in case you need a break."

"I need a break right now," he replied. "On my shrinking wallet."

"I'll try to keep the cost down," she said, glad he was tuning in to her ideas. "But if we do this, it has to be done right the first time. This house deserves our best efforts."

"The things you say," he replied. "Doing it

right the first time. Our best efforts. You truly are that kind of woman."

"What kind of woman is that?" she asked, confused.

"The kind who won't betray anyone."

With that he turned and marched back into the big central hallway. "Let's go upstairs."

Davina needed a drink of water. Did he distrust her so badly that he didn't even want to be around her? That would explain why he'd pushed her away when she only wanted to do the best job possible. *Business*, she told herself. *This is strictly business*. This man was so bruised and battered, she was surprised he could even function.

But he had to function. He had to keep moving.

And so did she. This house could give her the kind of professional recognition that most contractors only dreamed about. Then she and her crew could go from being a small-time company to becoming Davina Connell Renovations—her name for her one-day full-fledged company. Da would be so proud.

Her father had always believed he'd failed his family when his company went under several years ago. But if she made a name for herself, Davina could help him bring it back to life and get her brother Darren involved, too. If he'd quit being so stubborn about things. Darren worked hard to help Da, but he'd sure resented her going out on her own five years ago.

She'd wanted Darren to be her partner, but at the time her brother hadn't been ready for that. He'd been too caught up in his own heartbreak. Darren didn't believe that their father had suggested she strike out and find her own way. He thought she'd betrayed them all by leaving the fold. He still believed that.

What would Santo think if she told him that story?

Pushing her tumbling thoughts away, she followed Santo upstairs. He stopped on the wide landing. "I like this spot," he said, turning with hands on his hips in that Santo way.

"I thought I'd put another, smaller den and sitting area up here since the children will need some privacy as they grow older."

"Good idea." He moved down the hallway and they talked about the three bedrooms. "This one near the stairs will be good for Nate. We'll have to put up a childproof gate on the stairs, of course."

"Of course. If you're worried, we could take that extra room off the kitchen and make it his bedroom for now. It's technically a sitting room but since you rarely sit…"

"That might work," Santo said, giving her a

wry smile. "I worry he'll fall down the stairs. He's come close several times at the bay house but we did finally find a gate we could secure the last time it happened."

"I'll do some sketching," she said, making a note. "Meantime, we'll make sure his future bedroom is ready and waiting. You can use it for guests for now."

"Or Mrs. Brownlee," he said. "She has an apartment here in town but I might persuade her to move in. If things continue to go well with her."

"Yes." Davina smiled at that. "She doesn't talk about her past a lot but I do know she went to nanny school in England. I can't get her to say what she did before that, however. She's a very private person."

"There's a nanny school?"

"Yes. Do you know anything about her besides what you checked on when you hired her?"

"I only made sure she was fully vetted and would be good with my children. Rikki and Blain made sure of that but we didn't get a lot of details. She had excellent recommendations from past employers." He shook his head. "I've got to get into the game, don't I? Just saying that out loud makes me sound like an arrogant, distant father. I don't want to be that kind of man."

"You're not that kind of man," Davina said, joy bursting through her. "But yes, you might want to get to know the woman who's taking care of your children."

"I think you're right. We usually pass in the hallway or talk about instructions and schedules rather than personal things." He gave Davina a direct glance. "You and I talk more about personal things. Or at least, you drag it out of me."

"I'm not prying," she said in her defense. "I'm trying to get a handle on you so I can create a house that works for you."

"It's working so far," he said, his expression sheepish and surprised. "Amazingly."

Santo was beginning to see the whole picture. Her heart seemed to turn on her as the image of his family being happy here came to mind. That would make this a perfect home.

"I'm glad," she said. "I want this to work."

Davina would have to move on, but oh, the daydream of staying to witness that was way too tempting. The daydream of being a part of that threw her completely. Way too tempting. It couldn't happen.

"I'd better go," she finally said. "I've got lots to think about."

They went back downstairs and talked about landscaping and furnishings and several other aspects of renovation. Santo listened and asked all the right questions. She hated to leave now that they were finally communicating.

Thirty minutes later she'd stalled long enough and was headed out the door when Santo called her back. "Do you want to go grab a bite to eat?"

"You and me?" she asked, caught off guard.

"Yes, you and me," he replied. "The kids and Mrs. Brownlee are going to an early movie."

"Oh, well, then. I do need to eat. I don't have any cupcakes in my bag."

"I wondered when you'd whip one out," he said, his gaze moving over her face.

Davina's head told her to decline. But her heart was dancing around in a happy jig. "I... uh..."

"If you'd rather not."

"I am hungry," she said. "I only had—"

"A cupcake for breakfast and another for lunch."

She grinned at that. "I had a banana and some walnuts for lunch, thank you very much."

"That's not a meal."

"It is when you're too busy to eat anything else."

"So?"

"So, let me run by my place and freshen up and I can meet you somewhere."

"No. I'll go with you and wait out by the lake. We can walk to one of the cafes nearby."

"All right," she said, thinking about how strange it would be to come down from her little apartment and see him waiting for her. And then thinking about how she must look and wishing she had time to tidy up.

But he'd seen her worse than this. She wouldn't put on airs or mascara for this man. She couldn't let her heart overrule her head. She needed to get this job done and move on.

But one quick meal wouldn't hurt, would it?

Just another part of that daydream that she shouldn't be dreaming. One meal and then she'd get through tomorrow for the kids' sake. But come Monday, back to business.

Or at least she told herself that while she hurried to clean up and look presentable for a man who didn't have the heart to see beyond her carpentry skills long enough to even notice her as a woman.

Chapter Nine

Santo watched as she came back down the stairs. He'd stood here for all of ten minutes, looking up at the white church steeple silhouetted against the end of dusk and the beginning of night. Beyond the starkness of the steeple's spire, one by one, all the stars took their cue from the evening star and began to twinkle and wink down at the dark waters of the lake. The crescent moon lifted up into the night like a delicate sliver of gold, shimmering and unreachable.

In spite of all of that, he'd come close to leaving.

But he was tired of running from the things he didn't think he could handle and he was tired of running from the strong pull of Davina Connell and her tool belt. He had to do this. He had to help her restore the house he wanted to spend his life in, with his children. The letting go was hard for him but the freshness of being around her was intoxicating and enticing.

She'd lured him into believing he could make this work and he wanted to follow her and see it through to the end.

When he turned and saw Davina coming down the stairs, his heart, hard and bruised and shut off for so long, began that strange, exhilarating beat again. She looked the same and yet she looked different. She wore clean jeans and a lightweight blue open sweater over a white blouse. She'd taken her hair down from the usual haphazard bun. It hung in loose, riotous curls and waves around her face and shoulders.

And she smelled so good. Like a cluster of pure white magnolias hanging heavy from an old limb, like a spray of tiny jasmine blossoms floating on the night breeze. He'd never smelled any scent so sweet. It cleared his senses and made him breathe again, really breathe.

"I'm ready," she said, her tone timid, her eyes on him steady and searching. That statement seemed to become a challenge between them.

"It's a good night to walk," he said, not needing to fill the silence, but needing to affirm that they were actually doing this.

"Yes. One of those rare late spring nights

where the humidity has lifted. Clear and crisp." She looked up as the stars. "And that sky. I wish I could capture this time where the sun is settling down and the moon is taking over. I'd put it on a wall so I could see it every night."

Santo cataloged her request and decided he'd search for a painting that came close to what she wanted. It had been a while since he'd bought a gift for anyone other than his children.

"Where would you like to eat?" he asked, keeping a few inches of air between them.

"I don't know. Maybe something near the marina. I love seeing the boats coming home for the night."

They strolled along the boardwalk, speaking to strangers and people they recognized. When Santo spotted the quaint Lakeside Café, he motioned toward it. "French and discreet. Good food without being pretentious."

"Do you come here a lot?" she asked, those green eyes questioning.

"No, not much. I've had lunch with my parents here and I've brought a few clients here but I've never brought anyone here for dinner."

"I'm not dressed," she said as if to ward off the intimacy of his admission.

"You're fine," he replied. "It's casual. Look at the place. It's the oldest restaurant in town and it's on the marina. People come for the ambiance and the view."

She smiled up at him. "Okay. Now I'm craving French food."

Santo guided her underneath the blue-and-white arched awning leading to the restaurant doors. Several white wooden benches flanked by pots of saucy red geraniums lined each side, patrons gathered on some of them.

After he gave the hostess his name, he noticed the young girl's curious expression. "We'll be the talk of the town," he whispered to Davina as they sat down on one of the benches.

"Why?" she asked, glancing around.

"I'm an Alvanetti," he said, rethinking this whole dinner plan and wishing he had gone on home.

She shrugged and turned to stare down a few curious people.

"And I'm a Connell. It's none of their business."

"They make it their business," he said, wanting to shield her from the brutality he and his children had gone through.

She leaned close. "We can choose to ignore all that. Tell me what's good on the menu."

Santo shook his head. "Does anything ever get to you?"

"Many things. All the time. I hate it when

people neglect things or throw away perfectly good furniture. I like neat lines and a minimalist kind of decorating. I'm not good with clutter."

He absorbed that and then said, "Sometimes when you're talking about houses, I think you're not really talking about houses."

She gave him that secretive smile again. "And sometimes when you're talking about protecting your children, I think you're not really talking about protecting *just* them."

"You think I need protecting?" he asked, the quietness of being near her a nice contrast to the curiosity all around them.

"Yes, I do," she said. "From yourself."

The pager buzzed in his hand, its blinking red lights bringing them apart.

"This is going to be an interesting dinner," he said. But he was looking forward to talking to her, really talking to her. He needed to talk to people more. And starting with Davina seemed like the nicest way to form that habit.

Davina couldn't remember when she'd had a more relaxing meal. They'd dined on citrus chicken salad, crusty bread and a lemon-basil soufflé that melted in her mouth.

"That was incredible," she told Santo after she'd scraped away the last of the soufflé.

"It was a good meal," he replied. Then his lips turned up in a half smile. "I've never known a woman like you. You don't hold back on anything, including eating a good meal."

Davina put a hand to her mouth. "Oh, no. I'm not very ladylike. My mother tried to teach me manners but I do enjoy good food."

"No, you did nothing wrong and your manners are impeccable," he said. "I'm giving you a compliment. My wife, she ate like a bird. She liked being skinny."

Davina could see the old hurt in his dark eyes. "Skinny is not in my vocabulary," she said, hoping to keep things light.

"You don't need to be skinny," he said, his gaze touching on her and moving on. "You have curves."

"You've noticed?"

"I notice a lot of things," he replied, his smile simmering down into a daring but friendly smirk.

"Hmm. I'll have to remember that. You are observant but you don't share your observations."

"I learn things when I'm quiet."

She had to ask. "What have you learned about me, other than I can pack away food?"

"You're thoughtful," he said, giving her another thorough stare. "You have a sweet tooth."

"Yes." She pointed to the empty soufflé dish.

"You like children but I think you're not ready for your own."

That shocked her. "Why do you think that?"

"Because you came from a big family. You like the freedom of being independent. You don't want to be tied down."

That last part was wrapped in a tone of disappointment that caught at her like a tattered curtain. But she wouldn't tell him about how hard it had been when her father told her she needed to strike out on her own. "I have a lot I want to accomplish," she said, "but one day I'd love to have children."

She thought about his three. About holding Nate and rocking him to sleep. The little boy had captured her heart from the time Santo had thrust the crying toddler into her arms.

"I want children," she said on a somber note. "When the time is right."

"I'm glad to hear that," he replied. "I didn't mean to upset you."

"I'm not upset. You're right. But what I want right now is to continue renovating and rebuilding houses. I watched the house I grew up in slowly fall apart and I wondered why my dad, one of the best in the business, did nothing to keep it updated and working." Staring out at the water beyond the fancy sailboats and yachts lining the marina, she went on. "Later, when I was old enough to understand and after I'd made a nasty comment in front of my mother, she told me that my daddy was out there making everyone else's dreams come true because he couldn't make enough money to keep our dreams going."

"The cobbler with no shoes," Santo said, nodding.

"Yes. But he tried so hard to make it all work. I'm determined to keep working hard so I can repay him for teaching me my love for building, especially rebuilding. And one day, I hope to be able to renovate the home we all love."

Santo reached across the white linen tablecloth and took her hand. "I hope you can make that happen. I have dreams for Alvanetti Imports, too. Dreams that come by honest work and doing what's right. My wife didn't share those dreams. She didn't care if my family had a suspicious background or went about breaking the law. And I loved her too much to see her flaws."

"But you've worked to make it all right," she reminded him, not wanting to ruin their night. "I can see the good in you, Santo."

Pulling his hand away, he said, "Can you?"

"If you can see all you've mentioned in me, isn't it my turn to tell you what I see in you?"

"I don't want to hear what you see about me."

"Why do you dismiss your own good?"

"I don't want to talk about me. Up until now, this has been all about me. My houses, my children, my nanny, my family. I want to know more about you."

"You know enough," she said, leaning back in her chair, one finger moving over the gold etching on her coffee cup. "I love what I do and I'm trying to find my place in the world. In what is predominantly a man's world. I want to help my family, too." She wanted to make them proud.

"We share the same values when it comes to family. I'm trying to help my entire family get back on the right path, the good path."

"I can see that," she said, trying again. "I watch you with your children and you're a good father."

"You've only seen me recently," he said. "I haven't always been this attentive."

"We all learn from the past and work hard for the future," she replied. "I know you're doing that. So will you do me a favor?"

He gave her a look that told her she might be asking for too much. "What?"

"Don't be so hard on yourself. Remember, this can be the redo you need in your life. Go with it."

"So you want me to pretend when I'm still confused and grieving?"

"No, I want you to give up some of that control you hold so dear." Then she shook her head. "Let's just see how things go next week. Tonight, I want to enjoy that moon and those stars on the walk back to my place."

"Is that my signal to take you home?"

She tilted her head and shook out her hair. "I am tired. I've been up since five."

"Do you sleep?" he asked.

"Like a log. Most nights. But then, that's changed since I met you."

That brought a dazzling smile to his face. "Oh, so I keep you up at night?"

"Renovating your homes keeps me up at night," she amended so he wouldn't get the wrong idea.

Although, thoughts of this man did seem to find their way into her dreams.

He grinned and, thankfully, didn't pressure her on that.

They made their way outside and strolled along the boardwalk. Davina was full and content but her mind was in turmoil. Most of her clients were older and married, or younger and wanting a new house to start their lives. Happy people who wanted to create warm, cozy homes.

This man was different.

Tormented and brooding. Stubborn and proud. Lonely and distrustful. He was every romantic hero her sister Tilly had ever raved about. That alone should be enough to warn Davina away from him.

They walked in silence and spotted a blue heron standing still underneath a dock light. She pointed so Santo could see. "He's waiting for his supper. He can spot the fish in the shallows thanks to that light."

Santo watched the lanky, graceful bird. "I guess we all need a guiding light to spot sustenance, right?"

Davina pointed to the soft spotlight shining on the church steeple. "Yes, we sure do."

When they reached her little apartment, he insisted on walking her to the door. And there they stood, staring at each other, too much left unsaid between them.

"Thank you for going to dinner with me," he said, taking her hand in his. "I didn't want to go home to an empty house."

"I enjoyed it," she replied. "I guess I'll see you tomorrow."

"Oh, that." He looked as if he wished he'd never asked her to go to the festival with his family. "Bright and early. The girls will see to that."

"I get up early," she said. "Especially here where the light comes through the fan windows in the wee hours to wake me up."

His expression changed, intensified, brightened. "I'd think you must be beautiful in the early morning light."

Davina lost her breath. That image of waking up to a house full of running feet and dogs barking and life pulsing in pure joy around her caught her in a net of sweet imprisonment. She saw it there in his eyes, the same need, the same longing.

But before he could lean down and kiss her, she blurted, "You'd think wrong. I'm grumpy and unpleasant first thing in the morning. In any light."

For a moment, she held her breath and wished he'd just kiss her and get on with this. And he looked as if he felt the same way. His eyes went dark. Too dark.

Neither of them were ready for this.

"Good night, Santo," she said on a shuddering of breath.

And then she turned and hurried inside and

leaned back against the solidness of the heavy wooden door, not daring to breathe until she heard his footsteps echoing away from her.

Chapter Ten

"Why haven't you called?"

Davina glared at her cell for waking her up so early on a Saturday morning. "Tilly, it's six a.m."

"You never sleep late," her spunky younger sister said through a heavy chuckle. "Are you ill?"

"I *do* sleep late on the only day off I've had in three weeks," Davina replied through an irritated growl while she went in search of the coffeepot. "Or at least I'd planned to. Why are you up so early?"

"I miss you," her sister said on an exaggerated whine. "Da and Darren work all the time and Ma has been babysitting and dog-sitting to bring in some extra income. This big old house is lonely."

"Ma is dog-sitting now?" That was new.

Nancy Connell had always loved animals but Davina had never known her mother to take on extra dogs for pay. "Doesn't that make the house a little overcrowded since we already have two dogs and a cat?"

"No. She goes to some of the fancy homes in the Garden District and actually stays with the animals."

"Wow, that sounds interesting," Davina said, wide awake now. "How's Da?"

Tilly's voice changed from frivolous to serious. "He's working too hard. I worry about him. He and Ma seem at odds these days, too."

Davina had never known her parents to fight much. They were lovable and cuddly most days. "Is that why she's getting out of the house more?"

"Maybe," Tilly said. "I stay at my apartment most days but we all show up at the house when we want. But we miss you. That's why I'm worried about Da."

"Because of me?"

"Because of everything. You're part of it. He's a proud man and he doesn't like his daughter secretly sending money to his wife."

"He knows?"

"I think so."

Davina inhaled the smell of fresh-brewed coffee filling the air. "Well, I'm not going to stop but I'll figure out how to handle our father. I'm going to be here for a while so I can't deal with this right now. Three more months at least, but I'll send a check next week when I get paid for the first project. We finished the bay house yesterday."

"And how is it going, working for this mysterious Italian with three children?"

"That's a long story," Davina said. "And I haven't had enough coffee to tell it."

"Oh, this sounds good," Tilly replied, her tone full of questions. "I can wait for you to drain your cup."

"I'll have to call you later," Davina said. "I do have plans for this morning. Not this early but in a couple of hours. There's an art festival on the lake and I want to go. I'm going to buy Ma something nice for her birthday."

"Hey, I have a birthday, too," Tilly reminded her.

"I'm sure I'll find a trinket or two for you, too." Then she asked, "So what kind of mood is Alana in these days?"

"A dark one, as always," Tilly retorted. "She's never gonna get over breaking up with Lewis."

Davina's older sister Alana had always been moody and hard to read. But she'd dated the same man since high school and had big plans to marry him once he was through medical school. But once he was done, he'd suddenly called off the wedding and moved away with another woman. Now Alana, an RN, rarely came to family events and kept herself busy with work at one of the big medical centers in New Orleans.

"Well, they did date for seven years. He promised her the moon and left her in the dead of night."

"For another nurse," Tilly redundantly pointed out. "I can't reach her. You need to call her."

"She never picks up or returns my calls," Davina said. "But I'll keep trying. Have you heard anything from Quinn?"

"No. Deeply embedded somewhere in a dangerous place that I don't even want to think about."

"I'll say an extra prayer for him."

They talked almost an hour. Davina glanced at the clock and took one last nibble of the toast she'd popped into the toaster. "I have to go and get dressed. Santo and the children will be here at eight thirty."

"Wait? What did you say?"

Davina winced, realizing her mistake. "I said I have to go."

"No, the part after that. So it's Santo now, is

it? And with the kids, too. Are you going on a family outing with your client?"

Davina muttered under her breath. Tilly was like a dog with a bone. She wouldn't let go. "It's just the festival. He needs someone to help him keep them all together."

"Didn't you tell me he hired a nanny for that?"

"It's her day off."

"Right. You never date, Davina. Especially not with a client."

"It's not a date. It's a day in the park."

"That's a date in my book."

"Speaking of your book, are you still sweet on Axel?"

"Don't change the subject," Tilly said, her tone a little put off. "I want to hear all of it."

"I have to go," Davina said, again. "We'll talk later."

"Good. You'll have more to tell after spending the day with all of them."

Her sister ended the call. But Davina knew she wouldn't hear the end of this conversation. Tilly was right, however. She'd never before broken her strict rule of not getting involved with a client.

After last night, Davina wondered if she was doing the right thing by going to the festival with Santo. Would it send him the wrong message? She didn't even know what the message was anyway.

Or did she want to send him a distinctively different message than what her head was telling her. Could he sense that she was attracted to him?

Nervous and fidgety, she took a shower and dressed in denim capris and a sleeveless button-up blouse with a vivid wildflower print. After tying her navy sneakers, she tugged her hair into a loose ponytail and put on some lipstick and blush.

"This is crazy," she told her reflection in the bathroom mirror.

She kept talking to herself as she watered the plants and tidied up the little den. Out beyond the porch, the lake glistened and sparkled like a dazzling blue blanket. She could already hear the chatter moving between the vendors as they set up their tents along the shoreline. The smell of funnel cakes and barbecue merged to make her stomach beg to be fed again. The dry toast hadn't satisfied her but she didn't have time to go buy a muffin or cupcake.

By the time she heard a knock at her door, Davina had finished off three cups of coffee, two pieces of buttered toast and two small pieces of chocolate.

She was ready.

* * *

Santo wasn't sure how this was supposed to work so he'd sent Lucia and Adriana up to the door to get Davina.

But he watched with his breath held as the door swung open.

Surprise. She looked down to find his daughters standing there in their shorts and T-shirts, excitement making them dance and sway.

Confusion. She glanced down to where he stood with Nate, her eyes holding his in a silent question. Santo waved. Nate giggled and pointed. "Daddy, Dani."

Dani. She'd told him only her father called her that. How had Nate figured out her nickname? Or had his son found a way to say her name, toddler-style?

"Davina," he corrected with a gentle tone.

"Dani." Nate stuck to his guns with a pouting bottom lip.

Maybe he'd heard Davina and Mrs. Brownlee talking about their families. Those two did talk a lot.

He wondered what they'd said about him.

Too late to worry about that now. Davina and the girls were coming down the stairs. She looked prim and proper in her bright blouse and cute pants.

"Hi," he said, searching for a smile that he hoped would cover all of his insecurities.

"Good morning." She smiled back, hesitation in her words.

"It's a gorgeous day."

"Yes, it is."

"Daddy, can we ride the ponies?"

Lucia's question brought Santo out of the shell he was trying to stay inside. Like a tortoise, he lifted his head and stared around them.

The festival was in full swing.

Food trucks and drink wagons, booths displaying paintings and sculptures, jewelry and knickknacks. Some full of funky beach-inspired clothing and accessories and some full of books and photographs. Ice cream wagons and clowns and balloons and…life. This place was full of life.

Santo had forgotten what that was like.

Adriana squealed and pointed to the kiddie rides. "I want to ride all of them!"

Nate followed his sisters, squealing and pointing and asking for everything in sight.

Davina laughed and hurried to keep up. "They're wired."

"Yes," Santo said, watching the children and warning them to stay close. "They got me up early."

"My sister woke me with a phone call," she said, laughing.

"Do you talk to your family a lot?"

"As often as possible," she said. "She was checking up on me. She keeps me posted about everyone."

"Rikki does that for me," he said. "By the way, we've been invited over to Alec and Marla's house this afternoon after we've had enough of the festival. They're grilling and Rikki and Blain will be there, along with Preacher Rory and Vanessa. And maybe even Hunter Lawson and his new wife. They got married this spring."

"I've heard Marla mention all of those people," she said. "I haven't met Hunter and Chloe yet, though."

"Well, you might get that chance today."

"Do you want to go?" she asked, her question full of resistance.

"I didn't at first, no." He could admit that now. But he had to be honest with her. "I was an outsider around here for a long time but most of the people I know have been kind since everything fell apart. Rory has helped me a lot. I talk to him at least once a week. I'm teaching him how to play golf."

She glanced over at him. "And what is he teaching you?"

"How to find grace."

She looked pleased with that. "I've talked to him a lot, too, since I'm renting my apartment from the church. He's a good man."

"Yes." Santo wanted someone to say that about *him*. "Anyway, I can go to Alec's by myself or we can just hang out."

Another hesitant glance. "You don't have to drag me along. Are the children going?"

"Yes. Marla insisted. My girls play with her daughter, Gabby, a lot." Shrugging, he finally said, "We'll see how the kids are in a couple of hours. We might all need a nap."

Davina chuckled. "I'm thinking that chasing these three around is harder than putting up drywall."

They moved with the children, stopping for rides, face-painting and hot dogs, cotton candy and lemonade. Davina saw several pieces of art she liked and bought a few things for relatives and friends. By the time they'd gone through the whole thing twice, her tote bag was brimming with treasures and she'd made connections with several antiques dealers and art vendors.

They finally sat down at a picnic table by the water. Nate watched the boats coming and going while the girls fiddled with their new jewelry and some books Santo had bought.

Lucia got up to throw away some napkins.

"Stay close," Santo warned, pointing to a nearby trash can.

Then he turned to Davina and exhaled a long breath. "I'd forgotten what spending an entire day with these kids does to me. I'm both exhausted and rejuvenated."

"That's what children are for," Davina replied. "You have three precious ones, Santo."

"I know," he said. He finally looked her fully in the eyes. "I really enjoyed today. And last night."

She held his gaze and then dropped her head. "What exactly are we doing here?"

He lowered his head and looked up at her. "Eating too much junk food?"

She shook her head at his feeble attempt to dodge the real question. "You know what I mean."

Time to lay it all on the table. "I know what you're asking but I don't know the answer," he admitted. "I haven't thought of dating anyone since…since a long time. It wasn't on my agenda."

"Are we dating?"

"Do you want to go out with me again?"

"I don't normally get involved with my clients," she replied. "Never a good idea."

"Are we involved?" he asked, his head filling with what that could mean.

"Not yet," she said. "But if we're not careful, we could be headed that way."

"I can't explain," he replied. "Let's enjoy today and come Monday, we'll get back to work."

Her eyes filled with a bit of relief and a bit of disappointment. He shouldn't have blurted that out. But before he could explain, Adriana grabbed his arm.

"Daddy, Lucia's fighting!"

Santo stood and searched for Lucia. When he saw her a few feet away rolling on the ground with a little girl, he turned to Davina. "Watch Nate."

"Go," she said. "I've got him."

Santo lifted Lucia up and away from the angry blonde with the short bob. "What's going on here?"

Lucia was crying, sobbing and gulping, her face dirty and red. "She called Mommy a...a murderer. Tell her that's not true, Daddy."

"It is true," the other little girl shouted through her own sobs. "My mama told me not to play with you. Your mama was a bad person."

Santo held his daughter close and prayed for the right words. This was the same little girl who'd been taunting Lucia on the playground at school. He thought they'd cleared this up. But the other girl's mother rushed up to them before he could speak.

"What did your daughter do to my Beatrice?"

"I don't know what happened," Santo said, trying to explain without blurting out what the little girl had said. "They got into an argument."

"I know who you are," the woman shouted. "You had the principal call me to school because of your little brat there. You keep your children away from mine, you hear?"

Santo didn't respond. Instead, he held Lucia tight against him and searched for an escape from the crowd that had gathered.

And then he felt a hand on his arm. Davina, holding Nate in one arm and clinging to Adriana with her other hand. "Rory is here, Santo. He's taking us across the street to Alec's house."

Santo nodded and followed the preacher and Davina out of the park and across the street. He didn't stop or look back until he was inside the cool hallway of Alec and Marla's spacious Victorian house. But when he did turn, Davina was right there with him, his other two children still safe in her arms.

Chapter Eleven

Davina stayed seated in a comfortable side chair tucked away in the cozy open den, Nate asleep in her arms and a border collie named Angus curled up in a protective blob at her feet. She watched as Alec and Marla made sure everyone was okay. Marla gave the girls water and crackers and soothed them with soft words, her wheat-colored hair falling softly around her face. Her daughter, Gabby, and a cute white poodle named Roxie followed Marla around, helping.

The little dog wore a red vest indicating he was a service dog. He'd helped Gabby get over a traumatic event in her life, and now he was helping Lucia and her sister to forget what had just happened across the street.

But Davina couldn't forget it. Her stomach lurked and churned, her cheeks burned red with anger. She'd never liked bullies. Her parents had taught her to be tough but kind.

No matter what had transpired in the past, Santo and his family needed some kindness in their lives, and here in this house they were receiving it.

Rory and his wife, Vanessa, manned the grill outside and talked quietly to each other. Vanessa came inside with a platter of charred hamburgers and then turned to Davina. "Are you all right?"

"I'm fine," Davina said. "I just can't get that scene out of my head. It was horrible."

Vanessa sat down beside her. "Rory had a talk with Lucia. Only to reassure her that her parents love her and that her daddy won't let anything bad happen to her. She seems to think someone will harm her family." Lowering her voice, she added, "Apparently, this isn't the first time Beatrice has attacked Lucia. And her mother doesn't do a thing about stopping it."

"What did Santo say to Lucia?" Davina asked, a yearning to soothe him overcoming her.

"He told her that her mommy had gone through a difficult time and it had made her change into an unhappy person, but he assured Lucia that her mommy loved her and wouldn't want her to be sad."

And yet, the real question remained. How could he ever truly answer it?

Davina wanted to find that woman and child and have a good talk with them, but the woman would probably ignore her pleas. How could a grown woman be so cruel in front of a child?

Vanessa stood again. "Do you need anything? I'm going to check on the side dishes."

"No. I have some water." Davina indicated a tall crystal glass full of lemon, mint and ice.

Alec's aunt Hattie washed faces and placed the children's treasures away for safekeeping. She sent Davina encouraging smiles now and then, her pearls dazzling and her hair as shimmering gray-white as her jewelry.

"Can I get you anything, Davina?" she asked now, leaning over to touch a hand to Nate's forehead. "What a beautiful child."

"No, I'm fine," Davina said. "Maybe a place to let him sleep?"

"Of course," Aunt Hattie said. "Alec's office is across the hallway. The couch there is apparently quite comfortable, since I find him napping on it a lot."

Davina rose up, careful to hold Nate close, but before she could make a move, Santo, who'd been out on the back porch with Alec and Rory, came through the door and walked toward her. Then he gently took Nate from her, his tormented eyes locking on her. "I've got him."

"I was going to take him into the office and put him on the couch," she said, pointing across the house.

The look he gave her told her everything. A blank, empty stare that held a world of hurt and resolve. "I'm taking him home."

He turned and called to the girls. "Lucia, Adriana, let's go."

"Daddy, we don't want to leave," Adriana said. "Gabby says we can play with water balloons."

Lucia stood and gave him a look full of fear and determination. "I'm okay now, Daddy. If you want to stay." Her dark eyes grew big and misty. "I'm sorry."

"You didn't do anything wrong," he said. "But it's getting late and we should get home. Your brother is exhausted."

Davina glanced at him. "I can go with you—"

"No need."

With that, he took his children and walked out the back door to the side garden, obviously planning to take the back way to get to his car still parked at her apartment.

Hurt and hurting for him, Davina almost

went after him. Instead, she turned to Marla. "What should I do?"

Marla looked toward Alec, sympathy clear in her eyes.

"Let him go," Alec said. "He has to absorb this in his own way. He thought this had ended the last time it happened at school. And he wants to have a private talk with Lucia."

Marla sank down on the couch. "Lucia will be okay but sooner or later, he's going to have to explain to her what that girl was saying."

"Where are Rikki and Blain?" Aunt Hattie asked. "He needs his sister with him."

"Waiting for him at the bay house," Rory said, his tone quiet. "I've already called them."

Vanessa took his hand, smiling over at him.

Davina decided she needed to go home. No point in hanging around now. Santo didn't need or want her help and she was at a loss as to what she should do. Then she thought of the lake house and suddenly felt energized. She'd go there and work.

That was always a good way to find a solution to her problems. She'd take it out on old drywall and dingy carpet.

"I'm leaving, too," she said, smiling at the group gathered in the big room. "Thank you all for inviting me."

"Are you sure you won't stay?" Marla asked.

"My parents are coming and my dad really wants to meet you. I think my mom's been bugging him about remodeling."

Davina laughed at that when she wanted to run away. "Tell him I'd be glad to talk to him another time. I'm wiped out right now."

Marla nodded, an understanding in her eyes. "I will. Maybe when you're finished with the Alvanetti project."

The Alvanetti project was an understatement, Davina decided.

She said her goodbyes and walked home with a covered plate of food. But for once, Davina wasn't very hungry.

Santo had been better today—laughing, talking to her and opening up in a casual way that allowed her to get to know him in a new light. The kids had fun, too. They'd played, ridden fun kiddie rides and had done what kids needed to do, spend time with a parent.

Then, that terrible moment when the little girl's shrill accusations had echoed out over the crowd. She'd never forget the expression on Santo's face. Anger, despair and humiliation all caught up in a stony glare that dared anyone to touch his child again. It must have taken all of his efforts to keep from telling that woman to shut up.

He'd been dealing with this for so long now.

No wonder he needed a change. But he might need to consider if moving to the lake would keep this from happening. Surprised he hadn't just packed up and taken his kids far away, Davina put the food in the refrigerator and changed into her clean but old work jeans and a paint-spotted button-up work shirt and then she buckled on her tool belt.

Since she'd already had some of the crew drop off the other tools at the renovation house, she could easily walk around the lake, away from the festival, to get to the house. And she needed that walk to clear her head.

By the time she'd made it to the house, she could see the remains of the day across the water. The festival had died down and the few vendors left were loading up their wares. A gentle spring breeze danced through the palm trees as she crossed over by the rambling Tudor-style Millbrook Inn, where rumor had it that last summer Hunter Lawson had helped Chloe Conrad escape from two hit men who'd been hired to kill her.

So many people passing through her life had survived all sorts of life crises and had now fallen in love right here in this quaint waterside town not far from the Gulf of Mexico. She thought of Santo as she stood on the porch and stared out at the big lake.

And she knew in her heart, she didn't have a chance with him. Since she wasn't sure about her own feelings, she could handle that. What she couldn't abide was the pain and torment she'd seen in his eyes when his sweet little girl had begged him to tell her it wasn't true. That her mother wasn't a murderer.

He couldn't say that to his child. He wouldn't lie but he didn't know how to explain the truth.

And she didn't know how to help him. Except in the way she knew best. She could create a home that protected and shielded his children from the cruelty of the world. At least when they were within these old walls.

So she turned from the tranquil beauty of the sunset cascading out over the lake like spilled gold and concentrated on demolishing old walls and creating new open, tranquil spaces.

When she finally glanced up it was fully dark outside and… Santo was standing in the hallway staring at her with such a look of need that she dropped her sledgehammer and immediately rushed to take him into her arms.

He held her and breathed in the essence of her. Dust and a mustiness that spoke of aged walls and decades of footsteps, sweet florals and good, honest sweat that spoke of her commitment to this project. Santo didn't speak. He didn't have to with Davina. He held her and he let her hold him, their bodies tucked close to create a shield of warmth that made him feel safe, so safe.

Finally, he pulled away and looked down at her because he needed to look into her eyes. "You have smudges all over."

Reaching his hand to her skin, he gently traced the construction dust and wiped it away, his fingers finding the softness beneath the grit. "I'm sorry," he said. "I shouldn't have left you there earlier."

"It's okay." She put some space between them and wiped at her clothes. "Your children needed you."

"I needed my children." He glanced around and came back to her. "And I guess you needed to destroy some walls."

"Don't we all?" Then she asked, "How is Lucia?"

"Asleep," he replied. "Rikki and Blain are with them. And Mrs. Brownlee showed up and announced she's moving in."

"Good idea."

He felt the lump growing in his throat, swallowed, prayed he wouldn't break down. "People care about us, Davina. Good people care about my family."

She moved close again, one hand holding

his bare arm in what felt like his only link to reality. "Then remember that. Remember that you stayed here for your family, to rebuild the business so your children would have a good legacy instead of that one defining memory."

"But what if that one moment does define them? I can't always protect them."

"These people who care about you, they can define and protect your children. They will be with you all the way. Your parents will return soon and they love you and the kids. They'll help you. Rikki and Blain and now Virginia Brownlee will make sure your children are never alone. And Santo, I care, too. You have to see that."

He broke away before his emotions broke apart. "My children see that. Do you know that Nate calls you Dani?"

She gasped, tears forming in her eyes. "I rocked him to sleep the other day in…your room. He'd hidden there and when we found him, he got into my arms and asked me to rock him. Then he tried to say my name and I tried to teach him. But…he couldn't grasp it. He was drifting off when I told him to call me Dani. I didn't think he heard me."

"He heard," Santo said, his throat raw, his head hurting. "And he remembered."

She pushed at her haphazard hair and wiped at her eyes. "He's such a sweet little boy."

"I'm blessed," Santo said. "I wanted to keep them here but maybe I should leave Millbrook Lake."

"Are you thinking of doing that?"

He could see the disappointment and regret in her eyes. "I should have done it before things got too far out of hand. Before my children were exposed to the ugliness of it all." Then he shrugged. "But I think this will follow us no matter where we go."

She stood, looking like a fragile doll in the center of the big, empty room. But her gaze held a determined strength that no artificial doll could pull off. "Did you come here to tell me to quit?"

He shook his head, his heart gripped in a battle. "No, I came here after my children were asleep to look at what will soon be our new home." He paced again, staring up at the tall ceilings and the ornate chandeliers. "I came here to…pray. I asked God to give me a sign. Should I leave or should I finish what I started."

Walking back to where she stood, he touched a hand to her hair. "And then I saw a light on and I saw you, here alone, tearing things apart."

She moved closer, her fingers grabbing at his shirt, her eyes asking him to be honest. "And?"

"And I took that as a good sign. I'm staying."

Then he pulled her into his arms and kissed her, the taste of dust and decay mixing with the taste of sweetness and light.

He knew that sweetness and light would win out if he kept her near him.

Davina pulled away, surprise and what looked like awe in her glistening eyes. "Santo?"

"Give me that sledgehammer," he said. "I want to learn all about how to do a restoration."

Chapter Twelve

They worked into the night, talking some, not talking a lot. But getting to know more about this house and each other.

Around midnight, Santo's cell rang.

"Hello, Rikki."

He winked at Davina while he assured his sister that he was okay. "I'm with Davina at the other house. We're taking the first step. Demo."

Davina hid a smile, a sense of accomplishment and relief washing over her. After he'd kissed her, and after she'd recovered from the shock of need that had jolted through her at that kiss, she'd explained "demo" to him while his gaze had moved over her with a new awareness, while her heart had beat itself into that new awareness. Then they'd worked in silence, taking little breaks to discuss their plan for the house.

His plan.

Davina had to remind herself that this was Santo's home, not hers.

No. His plan.

God's plan, of course. This was out of her hands. She had to turn the future over to God and if that mean walking away, then she'd have to do that.

But when she heard Santo's soft tone, she prayed God would give her a sign, too. Glad that he'd calmed down, she knew nothing had been solved. He still needed to find a way out of his grief and pain and his children needed some sort of understanding of things.

He ended the call and looked at his watch. "I think we've done enough for tonight."

Had reality kicked in on him? Made him see he still didn't want to be here after all?

Davina ignored the disappointment of that possibility. "Is Rikki still at your house?"

"No. They left the children asleep and Mrs. Brownlee snoozing in a recliner. My sister was just worried about me. But when I told her I was with you, she seemed relieved."

That spoke volumes, Davina thought. Rikki's trust in her meant a lot to her. But she needed to process all that had happened today. "It *is* late and my muscles are screaming."

"How did you get here?" he asked. "I didn't see your truck."

"I walked," she said. "Never considered I'd have to also walk back this late at night."

"Nonsense, I'll give you a ride."

She brushed her hands off and then looked at her dirty clothes. "I'm a mess."

He tugged her close, his hand around her waist. "You look beautiful."

Davina smiled up at him and distanced herself from that attractive and rare happy look on his face. "Okay, we got a lot accomplished. Tomorrow we rest and then Monday morning my crew and I will get started on the big stuff." Pointing to the sturdy load-bearing column she'd left in place after they'd taken out the wall, she said, "We have to put up a support beam to make sure this open area is secure and once that's done I can take this column out. Then new drywall, updated fireplaces, all new doors and windows to hurricane-strength code."

Santo put a finger to her lips. "Stop. I'm so tired and you are making me even more tired. Let's go."

Davina pretended to pout but her chatter had defused the situation enough that she could resist his tempting kisses.

But when they got to his car, she shook her head. "I should have known."

A fancy sports car with the top down.

"I rarely drive it," he said with a sheepish shrug. "Rikki told me to get in it and put the top down to clear my head."

"And did it clear your head?" Davina asked, admiring the sleek black car.

"No, but being with you did."

He opened the car door for her, his dark gaze holding hers, a challenge in his expression.

Davina didn't speak. But she got in the car.

Sunday morning, a gentle rain fell as Davina walked the short distance to church, her umbrella forgotten back inside her apartment. Her muscles ached and she needed a good nap, but excitement coursed through her when she glanced across the way.

She could see the lake house located around the bend. The house that Santo and she had worked on last night.

Davina had worked on a lot of houses, mostly doing grunt work for construction foremen and before that, following her daddy around and asking too many annoying questions. Then she'd worked her way up the ranks until finally she'd bought her first flip three years ago with a loan from a small bank back in Bayou Fontaine. After a lot of sweat and angst and physical work from her daddy and her reluctant brother Darren, that house had sold and she'd made a tidy profit. Since then, she'd bought, renovated and resold four more houses. But this house, the lake house, would be her biggest challenge.

Her whole future was banking on making the lake house a true gem. Unless she got sidetracked by the handsome man who'd kissed her there in the demolished kitchen last night.

And kissed her again at the door of her apartment.

Can I do this? she wondered as she made her way up the slippery church steps. *Can I love the house and leave the man?*

"Whoa."

Davina looked up in time to see the preacher standing on the steps above her. "Oh, I'm so sorry," she said. "I need to watch where I'm going."

"I got you," Rory said, offering his hand to help her. "But you did seem somewhere far away just now."

"Not that far away," she replied on a wry note.

"Just across the lake maybe," he said with a knowing smile.

"You're too smart for your own good," she

retorted. "Yesterday was a strange day, full of all kinds of emotions."

"How did it end?" he asked, his expression serene.

"On a good note." She knew she could trust Rory. "Santo and I worked on the house until late into the night. Which explains why I need more coffee this morning."

"You know where the coffee is," he said, thankfully not asking for any more details. "And I think Marla dropped off breakfast cookies, too. You know, the ones that are supposed to be good for you, with oatmeal and less sugar and all kinds of healthy stuff but still worth the effort."

Davina knew the ones. "Thank you."

"Hey," he said as she was walking away, "I'm glad your night ended well."

"Me, too. Now I have just a few more weeks of praying every workday will end like that," she called back.

Davina made her way past the sanctuary and toward the kitchen at the end of the fellowship hall. But when she reached the open kitchen door, she heard a familiar voice.

"And that little brat had my Bea down on the ground, pounding at her. It scared me so bad, I'm still shaking."

The mother with the little girl from yesterday at the festival.

"I heard about it," another woman said. "But if Beatrice said those things—"

"Can you believe that? That little heathen is just like her mama, attacking Beatrice right there in front of everyone."

Another voice echoed out through the partially closed divider between the kitchen and the dining hall. "Well, maybe the child was upset."

"Why? Beatrice was telling the truth. Everyone knows what that woman did. It's horrible. I'm surprised those children haven't been taken away from that man."

Anger moved through Davina like a steamroller. She hurried through the door and glared at the woman and her two shocked friends. "You don't know me," she said, "but I was with the Alvanetti family at the festival yesterday and I heard what you said to Santo Alvanetti."

"It's none of your business," the red-faced woman said on a huff, her tone not so smug now. "And why would you want to be with a man like him?"

"He's a good man and he's my friend," Davina replied. "And his children have been through a lot more than most. He's trying to put his life back together. Could you please consider how fragile those children are? How it's not your place to shout out something like that in a public venue? Your daughter isn't to blame here since she obviously repeated what she'd heard an adult talking about, right?"

"My daughter is most definitely not to blame," the woman said, her hands on her hips.

The other women had moved away, clearly embarrassed. Davina knew she should leave it at that, but she had to defend Santo. "I'm only asking you to consider how your words not only affect his daughter but your daughter, too. It's not really your place, is it, to judge this family. What if you'd been through something like this? Would you want someone saying that to your child?"

"I'd never—" The woman stopped and looked behind Davina. "Well, that just figures. Now he's coming to church to find redemption."

The woman turned and hurried away, her skin beet-red. But Davina had seen a flash of regret in the woman's eyes, too.

Davina looked around to find Santo standing there with that tormented darkness back in his eyes.

Santo's stomach clenched. The coffee he'd had earlier now burned hot against his gut. Davina had defended him. And it made him even angrier than ever. She shouldn't have to do that.

Not here, of all places.

She hurried toward him. "I'm sorry, but someone needed to tell that woman to back off."

"You shouldn't have done that," he said, the good feeling he'd carried home last night now gone. "It's not your job to fight my battles."

She didn't even blink. "It is when someone like that doesn't see what her words can do to people."

"Let it go, Davina."

He saw the hurt in her eyes. And the determination. "So now you're angry at me?"

"I'm angry that you even have to defend me."

"I don't mind that, Santo. Let me decide that for myself."

"And let me take care of my own issues," he retorted. "You shouldn't get involved in this."

"I'm going to church," Davina said, her eyes downcast. "To pray for understanding. Because I'll never understand you."

Santo needed her to understand that he didn't want her good name to become tainted because of him. "Davina, wait."

But she was gone in a swish of skirt, her sandals clicking on the tiled hallway floor. Santo stood alone in the empty kitchen, wondering why he'd thought this was a good idea. He'd purposely left the children at home with Virginia to protect them, but now he had the added burden of keeping Davina out of the fray.

So he turned to leave, thinking he'd go home and tell Virginia to take the day off since she had a few more things to move to the spare bedroom, where she'd become an official squatter.

But his brother-in-law Blain Kent was standing at the other end of the big fellowship hall.

"Hey," Blain said, passing him by to grab some coffee. "What are you doing?"

Santo didn't want to explain. "I'm about to go home. Changed my mind. The woman who upset Lucia yesterday just got into it with Davina, too."

Blain's steady gaze didn't waver. "You're gonna let some misguided woman with an unchristian attitude keep you away from the service?"

"I had to keep my children away so why should I be here?"

Blain gave him that hard detective glance he'd seen so many times. "This is the best place for you to be," he said. "Hold your head up and I mean up, bro. Look to Him for your strength and your answers. The woman who has it in for you, she's dealing with her own issues. Without going into detail, I can tell you she's divorced and she has a teenage son who's acting out. His little sister is probably following his lead. That woman is frustrated and scared and she shields her own issues by gossiping about others. Right now, she's thankful that you're on the hot seat because that can deflect the spotlight off of her troubles."

Santo absorbed that information and then asked, "So that's supposed to make me feel better about what she and her daughter did to Lucia yesterday?"

"Nope," Blain said. "It's supposed to make you see that we've all got something. But He's got us all." He shrugged and gave Santo a hard stare. "I see it all when I close my eyes at night, Santo. I see your wife coming for Rikki and I hear the gun go off and I sit up in bed, my breath caught in my lungs. I have to live with taking your children's mother. And we'll have to deal with that for the rest of our lives. But He's got us. He will see us through. It won't be easy but we've got to stand firm on this."

Santo wanted to walk away. But Blain's blue-eyed gaze dared him to do that. He's been so caught up in his own pain, he sometimes forgot Rikki and Blain and how they'd discovered the truth about Althea and Victor and their criminal intent.

"C'mon," Blain said, his expression shifting. "Rikki will be glad to see you."

Santo shook his head and stared at Blain. "I really don't want to like you, you know."

"Same here," Blain said with a wry smile. "But like it or not, we're family now. And family sticks together."

Santo couldn't argue with that. Blain had been a good brother-in-law considering how he'd met Rikki and how he'd felt about the whole family before. Santo followed Blain into the sanctuary and held his head high. And when he went to sit down next to his sister, he saw Davina sitting there with her.

Their eyes met and she smiled at him, a tentative smile that asked a lot of questions.

"I'm sorry," he mouthed, hoping she'd forgive him.

She didn't speak. Her eyes said what he needed to know.

Davina was better at forgiving people than he was.

And once they were alone together again, he'd also thank her for standing up for his family.

Yet another quality about her that he admired.

Chapter Thirteen

Monday morning.

Davina took a deep breath as she and her five-person crew entered the lake house. "This is it, guys," she said, turning to face the four men and one woman who followed her all over the place these days. After they'd finished the bay house, she'd told them all to take a long weekend. Some had headed home and some had headed to the nearby beaches.

"You already started?" her right-hand man Kurt Martin asked, his eagle eyes moving over what had once been a wall.

Kurt didn't like to miss out on demo. He'd gone back to Alabama to see his wife and two boys for the weekend so now he was anxious to get started.

"Yes. I had some time Saturday night so I went to work."

"You worked on a Saturday night, boss?" Kurt liked to tease Davina about her nonexistent love life. "That's just not right."

"Yes, and I enjoyed every minute of it."

Too much, she wanted to add. One brooding, confusing man and two wonderful kisses too much.

"Well, you sure got a lot done," Josh, the college kid who was working with them until the end of summer, said. "Who were you mad at this time?"

Did they all know her that well?

"Nobody in particular," she retorted. "Just needed to burn off some energy."

"She missed us," Becky said, grinning.

"I did," Davina admitted. Becky was older than her and divorced but the woman knew how to swing a hammer. And she was an Amazon woman so none of the boys messed with her.

That left Adam and Howie, two brothers who wanted to work with her forever, according to what they told her after each job. They were in their early twenties and both had business degrees but they'd rather be in construction than sitting behind desks. They had aspirations of being on one of those home shows on television one day.

"So we need to get that support beam up and

these columns down," Kurt said, already anticipating what needed to be done.

"Yes." Davina went to the old counter. "Here's the new plan. You've all seen it before but just as a reference."

"An amazing house," Becky said, coming to view Davina's blueprints. "You'll do great, boss."

"So do I look that worried?"

"Something's bugging you," Becky said, her short blond hair curling in the humidity. "Or someone."

"I'm fine," Davina said. "I should have taken the weekend off myself but I didn't. If I go home, I get caught up in the family drama too much and usually wind up getting back to the job late. Didn't want to risk that chance with this one."

"Maybe you can go home Memorial Day weekend," Becky suggested with a knowing smile. "Get away from that burr in your bonnet."

"Maybe."

Davina hoped she wasn't blotching everywhere but the burn of kissing her handsome, troubled client on Saturday night and then making him extremely mad on Sunday had certainly stayed with her all weekend. She also hoped that Santo would stay away today. She was still confused about what had happened yesterday at church. Sure, he'd told her he was sorry for being so harsh with her after she'd confronted that woman. And yes, they'd sat together in church. But he'd left so fast after that, she had to wonder if the man would ever be able to look her in the eye again.

Too many mixed signals and she had too many other things to worry about anyway. So Davina did what she'd always done whenever she needed to work through a problem. She kept tearing away walls.

By the end of the day, they'd cleared out the kitchen and dining area, secured the new open space between them with a massive support beam and widened the opening to the big room across the hall that would soon be a family room. The house looked younger already, as if the letting go of some of the burden had lightened it.

"Okay, go get showers and dinner," she told her tired crew. "And rest. Tomorrow, we start on the stairs and the bedrooms."

They all left for their rooms at the Millbrook Inn, teasing each other, daring each other, their laughter moving through the breeze off the lake in sweet echoes.

Davina stayed behind to go over the details one last time, her mind filling with images of what the finished project would become. Her mind filling with images of three dark-haired children running down the stairs to greet their dad at the stained-glass front door.

"I see you had a lot of help today."

She whirled from the spot where the old sink had been and saw Santo across the hallway. Blinking to clear her head, she said, "My entire crew is back. I couldn't do this without them and the locals we'll bring in to help us."

"A lot goes into this," he said, making it a statement, not a question. "You even manage to create temporary jobs for people here."

"Yes, well, we need carpenters, plumbers and all sorts of journeymen." She wasn't in the mood to convince him again tonight. She'd plied her case, told him her plans and laid this gem of a house at his feet, hoping to give him hope, hoping to win him over so that he'd become a part of this in an all-inclusive way. But he still balked and walked out when he didn't like the situation and he was probably still fuming because she'd stepped into a battle that he considered his alone.

He moved across the space, his shoes hitting against the old floors with a purposeful stride. "I came to apologize."

She pretended to be studying the massive support beam. "For what?"

"You know what," he said, spinning her around, his hands on her arms. "For what happened in church. You were standing up for my children and me and I shouldn't have snapped at you. I didn't handle it very well."

Davina moved away and whirled. "I'm becoming used to your snappish ways, Santo."

"That's not good."

"No, but good to know, at least."

Frustration sparked in his eyes. "I told you in church I was sorry and you seemed to accept it. Are you going to make me suffer and beg for forgiveness or will you accept my apology?"

Davina couldn't put him through any more suffering. "I could do that, but I'm not that kind of person. Consider it forgotten. And consider me a ninny for interfering where I'm not wanted."

He didn't speak but his eyes told her she was wanted in a way that took her breath right out of her lungs.

"I'm sorry, too, Santo. And I forgive you but you have every right to be a little upset with me."

Relief washed through his eyes. "Well, you'll be glad to know I didn't sleep at all. I wanted to talk to you after church but I had an emergency at work and spent the rest of the day trying to put out administrative fires."

"I guess I'll have to accept that excuse," she said. Then she added, "I didn't sleep much either. I shouldn't have butted into your business. It won't happen again."

She tried to leave. Needed to leave. This man was infuriating and complex and troubled and…so kissable. Too much of a temptation.

But he held her arm. "I'm sorry. Blain had a talk with me and made me see reason and a whole lot of other things. The woman's name is Annette Pickett. Her daughter is Beatrice and she has a fifteen-year-old son who's having some issues and causing her a lot of problems. She's afraid he'll turn to a life of crime. She's going through a bad divorce. Blain didn't give me all the details but after he told me some of her problems, I found out who she was and where she lives."

Davina's eyes went wide. "Are you going to confront her?"

Santo let go of her arm, his eyes filling with surprise and disappointment. "Do you think I've hired a hit man or that I just might scare the woman? Shake her down a bit?"

"I didn't mean that," Davina said, realizing how her question sounded. "Santo, honestly, I didn't mean it that way."

"But you thought it, right?"

"No. Maybe. You were telling me you'd

found out about this woman and you had all of her information. I jumped to the wrong conclusion." Then she put a hand to her mouth. "That's it, isn't it? You purposely didn't confront her at the festival because you knew people would jump to the wrong conclusion. And that's why you were aggravated with me yesterday?"

She leaned into the now-hollow counter support. "I never considered how that could cause a ripple effect."

His reaction made her see how much restraint he'd been using. Anger, followed by disappointment, a minute of staring at her and then…a long exhale. He'd been fighting this, too. Learning to control his anger so people wouldn't continue to judge him wrongly. She had to wonder how many times he'd turned the other cheek for the sake of his children.

"I can see how you'd get the wrong impression," he said. "And you know something? I can't blame you or anyone else. I can't even blame Annette Pickett or her little girl. I think the shadow of my family's reputation will always be over me, no matter what."

"No. Not if you keep doing what you need to do to make it right," Davina said. "So what are you going to say to this woman when you contact her?"

"I'm not planning on saying anything to her," he explained. "But I know she's looking for a better-paying job and I have several openings at the store and in the warehouse."

Davina didn't hide her surprise. "A good idea, but she might spit in your face."

"I won't be the one offering," he said. "Rory's going to mention it to her."

"And if she says no and spits in his face?"

"Then I've done all I can do."

"And what about Beatrice and Lucia? They have to go to school together."

"I talked to the school officials today and Lucia and Beatrice aren't in the same classes so they rarely see each other and they have different recesses now. I think Beatrice heard her mother talking about us at the festival and said something to Lucia only because it was fresh in her mind. Her teachers are aware of the situation, but it will be up to her mother to change this."

"How is Lucia?"

"Better. We had a long talk when I got home yesterday afternoon, just she and I." He paced the floor and touched on the exposed walls. "I told her that Mommy got confused and made some decisions that caused her to get in trouble and she hurt a lot of people but that none of that is Lucia's fault. I tried to explain that

Althea's death was a tragic event and that none of us wanted it to happen. I also told her that she and I are going to talk to someone who can guide us through this. A new counselor Rory suggested."

Davina wanted to hug him tight. She could see the fatigue circling his eyes like a dark aura. "I'm glad to hear that. I can't imagine how hard this has been for all of you."

"It will always be hard," he said. "One day, they'll all know the truth and then Rikki and Blain will have to deal with it even more. It won't end, Davina. Ever."

She didn't miss the warning in that statement. "Is that why you keep pushing me away?"

"Do you think I'm pushing you away? I mean, you have a life and you have plans. Why should you want to get involved with someone like me?"

"Maybe you don't want to get involved with anyone at all," she replied. "You didn't like me coming to your defense and you're still mad about it, even after both of us apologized."

He gave her one of those doleful, dark stares that said everything but told her nothing. "I'm mad about life in general but you will never understand how it felt to see you rush to my defense. No one besides my family has done that. Not in such a bold way."

"I can be bold," she said, walking up to him. "I fight for what I believe in and I believe in you."

"Why?"

"Because I've seen you in action, Santo. You have integrity and grit and you want to do what's right. You'd do the same for me."

"But these days I have to walk away. I can't fight. It would only set things back."

"Or set them straight," she countered.

He pressed his hands against the skeleton of what used to be cabinets. "I came by to tell you how sorry I am for taking my frustrations out on you yesterday. And I wanted to let you know that I'm taking a couple of weeks off from work to help with this project."

Davina shook her head. She was tired and she needed a shower but all she wanted to do right this minute was hug Santo close. "You are full of surprises."

He laughed, a low growl of a sound because technically, he never did really laugh. "Is that okay? Me hanging around with a hammer?"

"Depends," she said, walking toward the back door. "I'll have to see your skills."

"Oh, I have skills. I'm only just beginning to show you my skills."

"Right." She checked the empty, echoing room, her mood decidedly better now. "Let's go. I need to get cleaned up and find some dinner."

"Okay. I'll wait for you at your place."

"You don't have to do that. I wasn't fishing for us to eat dinner together."

"Yes, I do. Virginia wants you to come over to our house for a proper meal."

Davina thought about that. "How thoughtful of Virginia."

"Yes, isn't it, though?"

"But you don't need to wait. I can meet Virginia at your house."

"No, I will take you and drive you home."

"Did Virginia suggest that?"

"No, that's all my idea. My plan is to have you alone for at least fifteen minutes each way."

"Sports car? Top down?"

"Yes. It's a nice evening out."

"In that case, give me about twenty minutes."

He nodded, clearly relieved and pleased with himself. "I'll go visit Rory and Vanessa while I'm waiting. How's that?"

"Good idea." Because she'd be a wreck knowing he was sitting in her living room or hanging out on her porch.

"Let's go then. I'll follow you to your place and give you exactly twenty minutes before I come looking for you."

Davina knew he meant that. And she had a feeling they'd just turned a very important, very intimate corner.

But she sure couldn't predict what they might encounter down the road. Only prayer and God's grace could reveal the future. She'd have to trust Him to show her which road to take.

Chapter Fourteen

"Hello, Davina."

"Hello, Virginia."

Santo watched as the two new women in his life exchanged pleasant greetings, their expressions as serene as the water down in the bay.

"Thank you for inviting me to dinner," Davina said, her gaze moving over the house she'd renovated. "You've got the place looking good."

Santo followed her gaze. Color shined brightly in the glow of the new light fixtures she'd had installed along the big oval hop-up bar that occupied a huge space between the kitchen and the den. More color brightened the spacious den in pictures, drapery and rugs. A still life of sailboats in the bay hung over the massive fireplace, mirroring the real bay outside.

Warmth. This home now had a warmth that had been missing before. One wall in a discreet corner held black-and-white photos of the children, laughing and running, right along with colorful portraits of each one in a more formal setting.

Althea had never bothered to display them. She'd kept them hidden away in a box in a storage closet, always saying she would let Rikki do something with them one day.

That day had never come.

But he was here now, with Davina.

She had certainly brought more than just warmth into this house. She'd breathed a new life into his whole family. He'd miss her when she was gone.

"Daddy!"

The sweetness of his children hurrying toward him brought Santo the kind of peace that made him thankful for each breath he took. "Hello!" He grabbed up Nate and tickled his tummy and kissed his cheek. Then he did the same with Adriana. "How did your day go?"

"Good," Adriana said, bobbing her head. "Miss Virginia let us swim and she showed Nate how to hold his breath."

Nate demonstrated with puffy cheeks and mischievous eyes.

Lucia stood to the side. "I'm learning how to do a flip, Daddy."

"That's great," Santo said, nodding at Virginia. "Our new nanny is a woman of many talents."

"I was a champion swimmer in college," Virginia stated in a matter-of-fact way. "I'll have them all acting like little fish before summer is over."

Davina turned to Santo and took Nate out of his arms. "I've missed all of you so much."

Nate giggled and poked her in the cheek. "Dani."

"Dani," she said, nodding, her gaze meeting up with Santo's.

Lucia tugged at Davina's crisp white blouse. "We just saw you on Saturday. That means you missed us for almost two whole days."

"I sure did," Davina replied with a grin. "Two whole days of not seeing you."

"Seems longer," Santo interjected and then wished he hadn't when Virginia grinned.

"I missed you a million-gazillion," Davina retorted with a wink to Nate. She put him down and turned to Virginia. "What can I do to help with dinner?"

"Not a thing," Virginia said. "The children and I have it well in hand."

Davina looked surprised and pleased. Santo met up with her near the glass wall out to the pool. "I guess you saw the for-sale sign in the yard. Rikki listed it today."

"I did notice that," she said, giving him a focused stare. "How do you feel about that?"

Remembering his earlier conversation with Rory and Vanessa, he said, "Good. Like I'm finally coming out of a dark fog." He told her that Rory had set up a meeting with Annette Pickett to counsel her. He hoped Santo and Annette could meet in the next week or so and resolve this issue with their girls. "That's part of why I wanted to talk to Rory. We can't start over if Lucia is still being harassed and bullied."

He shook his head. "I told him when I watched Rikki put up the sign, I almost stopped her. But then I thought of you and the new house and how hard your crew worked both here and now there. Change isn't easy, is it?"

"No. I've seen a lot of people during this kind of transition process. There's so much emotion that goes with a for-sale sign. Each one has a story behind it, sometimes good and sometimes not so good."

"You're not like any contractor I've ever known before," he told her. "I've never looked at houses in that way. All wrapped up in emotions and tough decisions. I just always saw the housing market as a sign of progress. Now I see things so differently."

"Buying something that takes a lot of attention and income is always an emotional and stressful endeavor," she replied. "But I love being a part of the process."

His eyes met hers. "You picked the right profession."

She glanced around when the children started laughing and talking and saw Virginia demonstrating with exaggerated clarity how to butter bread. "Seems like she did, too. She clearly adores your children."

He let out a sigh. "Yes, I have to admit the morning you both walked into my life has changed our world."

"It's just beginning," she said. "This is a beautiful place but change can be good."

"I'm seeing that," he said, a soft smile on his face.

Virginia motioned to them. "Dinner in five minutes."

"It smells so good," Davina called out. "I'm starving."

"Chicken pot pie and salad, with lemon bars for dessert," Virginia said. "And the children helped with everything."

Davina walked into the kitchen and grinned at the girls and ran her hand through Nate's always-messy hair. "I'm impressed."

Santo guided her into the dining room where the changes she'd made seemed to bring the tropical yard right into the room. Parlor ferns and bird-of-paradise plants sitting in the corners and a bright, floral rug underneath the teakwood table. A comical portrait of a parrot sitting in a jungle on the wall.

Before this room had been sterile and unwelcoming, with the bare table and some sort of twisted sculpture clinging to the wall like an old vine.

The children loved this room now. He did, too.

As they sat down to dinner and joined hands to say grace, something Virginia had incorporated into each meal, he thanked God for these two remarkable women.

He prayed that Virginia would never leave and he prayed that he'd be able to let Davina leave.

Later, Davina insisted on helping Virginia with the dishes.

"You're a good cook," she said, wondering about Virginia's past. "Where did you learn?"

Virginia gave her that Mona Lisa smile. "Here and there. I worked a lot of odd jobs before I settled on taking care of the wee ones."

"How long have you been a nanny?"

Virginia's smile seemed to slip. "Close to twenty years now."

Davina didn't press for any more information on the past. Instead, she looked toward the future. "So you're living here now?"

"Yes." Virginia dried the baking dish she'd used to cook the pot pie. "When I heard what had happened at the festival, I thought they might need me more than just seven-to-seven. I'm alone and I don't mind. Just made sense."

"It does make sense. Are you moving into the lake house with them?"

"I hope," Virginia replied, her gaze searching for the children across the way. "The little stinkers have embedded themselves into my heart."

"Good," Davina said. "I have the perfect suite of rooms for you. Near the kitchen and near a room where Santo wants to put Nate until he's older."

Virginia didn't speak but the glistening mist in her eyes showed Davina that she needed this family as much as they needed her.

"I had a nice time," Davina told Santo after he'd pulled the sleek sports car into the tiny gravel drive up to the garage apartment. "Virginia is an interesting woman."

Santo stared at the dark lake waters. "Yes, but she won't talk about her past. It's strange but I trust her. Which is unusual for me."

"Rikki had Blain did a background check, right?"

"Yes. I asked Rikki about that the other day

since I didn't get all the details before. Virginia passed the check with flying colors. She went to nanny school in England, just as you told me." Then he turned to face her. "But…do you really want to spend our last few minutes together tonight talking about Nanny Mod-Squad?"

She had to giggle at that. "She does remind me of someone out of a seventies' sitcom."

"Another bright spot in a house that had lost its luster."

Davina's heart seemed to be casting out a line but she wasn't sure she was ready to grab this catch. "Santo, are you okay? I mean really okay?"

He held to the steering wheel and stared up at the full moon hovering like a lost beach ball in the sky. "I'm getting there, yes." Then he slanted his body so he could see her better. "Are you afraid of me?"

Davina's mouth dropped open. "Afraid of you? Why would you think that?"

"You seem unsure about me."

"I am unsure, about a lot of things. I've never done this before."

His eyes turned onyx. "What? Sit and look at the moon on a beautiful night?"

She slapped at his arm and he grabbed her hand. "I've looked at the moon a lot, but never with someone like you," she admitted. "I'm not sure what to make of you."

"Do you have a boyfriend? I should have asked you that a long time ago, huh?"

"I've dated off and on," she replied, the warmth and strength in his hand holding her steady. "Work tends to get in the way of anything lasting."

"I could use that same line on you," he retorted. "So that excuse won't work on me."

"I don't have any excuses. Just concerns."

"And I ask again—are you scared of me?"

"I'm scared of how you make me feel," she said, the touch of his fingers against her sure and secure even while her heart was racing in a frenzied confusion. "I told you, I've never done this before. Of course, most of my clients are either retirees or young couples. Sometimes, big families needing more space."

"I'm different that way."

She glanced over at him and saw the smile in his eyes.

"That's different," she said.

"What?"

"You've changed since the first time we met. You've lightened up."

"Oh, so you've noticed. How else have I changed?"

"Your eyes didn't smile before. Now when you look at me, your eyes seem bright and aware."

"I am very aware of you, I can tell you that."

She basked in that admission. "I mean, you're more aware of everything—what needs to be done, your children, the nanny. Me."

He laid his head back against the headrest. "I guess I'd forgotten how to really smile. So that scares you?"

"No. That's a good thing."

"But?"

"But I don't know how this will end." She turned to stare over at him. "Before, it's been simple. I come in and renovate and spruce things up and then I hand over the keys, get my check and leave. But with you, I can't be sure of the end."

"I'm not so sure of the end of this either," he replied. "But for now, can we just go with what's happening in the moment?"

Turning the tables, she asked, "Are you scared of me?"

"Absolutely," he said. "Completely."

Then he kissed her, his arms wrapped around her. "You terrify me," he said after he'd sat back to look at her. "There are so many reasons I shouldn't be here with you."

"Yes, I agree."

"So we agree we shouldn't be doing this and yet we can't seem to stop doing this."

"It's a problem."

He kissed her again. "But I have three very good reasons to want to keep you near."

"Only three?"

"Yes. Lucia, Adriana and Nate. They seem to like you a lot."

His words touched her so deeply, she had to take a breath. "I like them, too. A lot."

She loved his children but if she mentioned that word, things could take a definite twisting turn.

"Do you like me? A little?"

"Yes," she said. "I do."

"So for now will you please stop being scared of me and let me be a part of renovating the lake house?"

"Are you kidding me? I want you to help there. You know that."

"Yes, but you want me for professional reasons. I want to be there for personal reasons."

She leaned close and whispered, "I told you this would get emotional. It's all about personal reasons."

"It got emotional the day I handed Nate over to you."

Davina kissed him this time, turning yet another corner, taking a detour that had warning signs all over it.

"I'll see you bright and early tomorrow morning, Santo," she said. Then she hurried to get out of the car. "If you think I'm scary now, wait until you've been through a whole day of renovations with me."

He laughed at that but she heard the edge in that laugh.

He truly was terrified of change. And that meant they might have to end this before it ever really got started. This attraction could only carry them so far before they'd have to get to the bones of this budding relationship. The whole thing could cave in on them if they weren't careful.

Chapter Fifteen

"I'm yours for at least the next two weeks," Santo told Davina the next morning.

Tilting her head, she gave him one of those questioning glances. "You might live to regret that."

The sun was up, bright and sure. The day held little humidity but already, he could tell it would be warm.

Each time he glanced at Davina he turned warm. "I'm not completely helpless in the handyman department," he said. "We're always hammering and fixing things around the warehouse."

"That's cute," she said with a mischievous grin.

Santo wondered if he truly would live to regret this. Being around her day in, day out could prove to be his undoing.

These foreign feelings had kept him up last night and given him time to reflect on his life and what he wanted from here on out.

His children. His family. A quiet life. An honest life. Honest work. And someone like Davina in that life.

And yet, he didn't feel he had the right to tug her into the jarring spotlight of being around the mighty Alvanetti clan. So he'd decided he needed to back off on the top-down drives and the over-the-top kisses. The woman should be able to do her job without worrying about him all the time. She had big plans for her future. He could give her exactly what she wanted. He'd give her a glowing recommendation and a great review. He'd refer his few remaining friends to her.

Davina would make it big in the real estate and construction market. And he could try to forget her and get on with his own life.

"Are you ready for this?" she asked, passing him a cup of coffee.

"I'm not sure. What do you want me to do?"

"Mainly, stay out of the way," Kurt said in passing, a grin on his face. Then he shook Santo's hand. "Good to have you here, Mr. Alvanetti."

The brothers Adam and Howie whizzed by, nodding a sleepy-eyed hello.

Becky came in and looked around, her hands on her hips. "Oh, good. A rookie. Always love me a rookie on the work site."

"I detect sarcasm," Santo said with a smile.

"You detect right," Becky answered. "But I promise I won't nail you to the wall."

"She knows how," Josh said, shaking his head. "Watch that one, Mr. Alvanetti."

After they'd all gone on to get started, Santo glanced around and then back to Davina. "Do they all know…about me?"

She gave him a direct stare. "They only know that we don't discuss clients or their personal lives on the job. We do our work, consult each other when we have problems and keep moving. You don't have to worry about any of them harassing or annoying you."

"Refreshing," he said, already feeling out of place but also impressed with her no-nonsense work ethic. "I'll ask again. What do you want me to do?"

"We're going to pull up carpet and see if we can salvage the wooden floors," she said. "Just follow my lead."

"I can do that," Santo replied. "I think."

Three days later, he hurt all over. But Santo had to admit, showing up here every day and being a part of this tearing down and rebuilding did have a therapeutic effect on him. Rory had told him physical labor was good for the body and the soul.

Or maybe being around Davina had a lot to do with his new attitude.

"It's lunchtime," Davina called. He followed her to where they all washed up with a water hose attached to a spigot near the back porch. "I think Kurt is looking for a nearby place to order takeout since we're so dirty and sweaty."

Santo was definitely dirty and sweaty. Sitting down on an overturned bucket by the old chair she'd pulled up near the front porch railing, he said, "I haven't been this tired or dirty since I used to work in the warehouse after school. Mandatory labor, according to my father."

"Tell me about your family," she said, grabbing an apple and a cold bottle of water.

They talked a lot on the brief lunch break, but usually it was about the crew or the work or her family back in Louisiana. She'd never pestered him much for information.

"You know a lot already," he replied. Then he gave her the quick version of how far the Alvanettis had come. "I run a clean operation. And from everything we can tell, so did my father once he turned his life over to God. Blain's father was a big influence on him."

"And Blain's been the same with you, it seems," she said with a soft smile.

"Well, when your brother-in-law is a detective…"

"Hey," Kurt called out. "We're ordering catfish from that place out on the main highway. You want in?"

"I'll take a single filet plate," she replied. "Santo?"

"The same," Santo said. Then he stood up. "Hey, Kurt, let me buy today, okay?"

Kurt glanced at Davina. She nodded. Santo pulled out several twenties and handed them to Kurt.

"Be back in a few," Kurt called with a wave. He and the brothers hopped into his big truck. Becky and Josh stayed behind to toss old carpet and other debris into the Dumpster they'd rented for the duration.

"Ready to throw down your hammer?" Davina asked, grinning at him. "I'm impressed that you keep coming back for more."

She had no idea. "No. But I need two pain pills."

"We have plenty of the over-the-counter stuff around."

"I'll take one after lunch." He drank his water and stared out at the lake. "This really is a nice spot. I hope the kids will make new friends here."

"I'm sure they will. Gabby is right down the street. She's a sweet little girl."

"Yes, she is. And her stepfather has a lot of influence in this town."

"Do you hope to cash in on that?"

So she still wasn't sure about him. "I hope he'll continue to be my friend."

His cell rang and he stood to dig it out of his pocket. "Time for my daily check-in with my manager at work. I'd better take this."

Davina checked her messages. One from Ma. Two from Tilly. And one from Alana. Hmm. Alana never called.

She hit her older sister's number and waited for her to answer. "What's up, Alana?"

"I'm worried about Da," Alana said without preamble.

"Why? What's wrong? I talked to Ma two days ago and everything seems fine."

"He's not doing well. He and Darren are struggling. They've been at odds for months now, and you're off doing your own thing as usual."

"Alana, what are you talking about?"

"Dad won't ask you to come home, but he needs you. You should know that."

"I'm calling Ma," Davina said before ending the call. Her absent sister had some nerve since she was mad at the world in general but took it out on her family. But if Alana was correct, Davina would have to go home immediately.

"What's wrong?" Santo said, obviously seeing the worry in her eyes.

"One of my sisters. She says my dad is sick and needs me."

Santo touched a hand to her arm. "You should go."

"I will, once I get the whole story." She moved away. "I have to call Tilly. She'll tell me the truth."

"Hey," he said, rushing after her. "Don't worry about this. Can your crew work without you?"

"If they have to, to get it done."

"And will they mind if I help out?"

"Not if I tell them to work with you."

"Then you do what you need to do and we'll take care of the rest."

Davina nodded and hurried away to call Tilly, her prayers now centered on her family back in Bayou Fontaine.

Santo sat with the crew, their food barely touched, and waited for Davina to come back from the far end of the yard.

He'd watched her pacing back and forth for a half hour now. When she finally ended the phone call and headed toward them, he could tell she'd been crying.

"He's in the hospital," she said, holding up a hand. "They took him this morning but he wouldn't let anyone call me. Not even Ma. I'm so angry I could kick something."

Kurt sent a bucket her way. "Go ahead."

Her eyes flared and she sent a booted foot straight into the hard plastic. The bright blue bucket went flying across the yard.

"Feel better?" Kurt asked, gentleness in his tone.

"A little." Davina let out a sigh. "I'm going to drive over there as soon as I can get cleaned up."

"You shouldn't go alone," Becky said. "I can go with you."

"No, I need you all here," Davina replied. "Now that we're down to the bare bones, you can get going on the trim work and painting. The paint is waiting at the hardware store. Kurt, you have all the information."

"We'll be fine," Kurt said. "You've laid out the plans. We know what to do. And I'll call you if we're not sure." Then he put his hands on his hips and gave her a fatherly smile. "Darlin', this ain't our first rodeo."

"*You* could go with her," Becky said, pinning Santo with a level stare.

Had her crew picked up on things between them already?

Davina shook her head. "Oh, no. I don't need anyone with me." Giving Santo a warning glance, she said, "No."

Santo would be glad to drive her up to see her folks, but it didn't look as if she'd agree to that. "I don't mind," he said. "But only if she wants me with her."

Davina looked over at him, worry and fear in her eyes. "It's four hours. I've driven it alone lots of times. Besides, I thought you wanted to stay here and work."

"I'll do whatever you need me to do," he replied. "I can drive you over to New Orleans and I can hop a flight home so you can stay. Then you'll have a car there."

"Good plan," Kurt said. "Then Mr. Alvanetti can come on back if everything's okay and help us here."

"Call me Santo," Santo said, a sense of relief settling over him with Kurt's approval. "Davina, how do you feel about that plan?"

"I don't need a babysitter," she retorted, anger clear in the declaration. "I'll be fine."

"No," he said, his hands on her arms. "You need a friend."

Davina glanced around and then back to him, a surrender softening her eyes. "Okay, you can go with me. But you're not staying."

Davina didn't know what to do or say.

"You'll have to leave your children," she told Santo after she'd come back to her senses later that day. "I can take care of myself. I've driven this route so many times I can do it in my sleep."

"The kids will be fine," he said. "Virginia knows what's going on and she agrees. Rikki is nearby and Marla has offered her help. Rory is praying for your family and he's coming by the house tonight to visit with the kids. We've got it all under control."

"Why are you doing this?" she asked, tossing an overnight bag into the covered tool-box in the back of her truck. Because she'd refused to take his sleek sedan or that too-obvious sports car.

"I told you," he replied, his tone firm. "You need a friend right now."

"I could get Vanessa or Rikki to go with me."

"They're both busy. I have two weeks off."

"To work on your house."

"I've worked for three full days now. And I'll take the red-eye back tomorrow and get in some more sweat equity. We both have to learn to trust other people, Davina."

"I do trust people. You're the one with that issue."

"It seems I'm not the only one," he pointed out as she backed out of the churchyard and headed toward I-10.

Davina let out a breath and watched the late afternoon traffic. "I trust my team. I'm worried about my dad. I'm upset that they didn't call me right away."

"They didn't want to scare you."

"No, Alana and Darren are angry at me. They think I've abandoned the family for my own ambitions."

"Do they know you send money home?"

"How do you know that?"

"I was guessing based on some of your comments," he said, looking sheepish. "You do what you can. You said your dad always encouraged you to strike out and follow your dreams. It sounds like he encouraged all of you to do that. You can't change how your siblings feel about things. Rikki stayed away from our family for years because she thought we'd caused her first husband's death. He was driving drunk and had a wreck. But she didn't know that. My father didn't want to cause her more pain but he finally told her the truth."

"Do you think there's something more to what's going on with my family?" she asked, her mind whirling in turmoil. "I should have gone home last weekend."

"I think you feel guilty but you shouldn't. You're not that far away at any given time. Your sister is going through her own thing, just like the woman who was so rude to Lucia and me at the festival."

"Have you talked to her yet?" Davina asked, to take her mind off her worries.

"No, but Rory is counseling her and he's mentioned me. I don't think she's ready to come around yet."

"People can be so stubborn." She stared at the road, her hands tight on the wheel.

After they'd gone a few miles, Santo pointed. "Stop here."

"You need a rest stop already?" she asked. "At this rate it'll take us till midnight to get to New Orleans."

"Pull into the parking lot, Davina," he said, his tone commanding.

She did as he said, thinking he wasn't a very good traveler. But Santo surprised her yet again after she'd parked the truck. "Now get out and come around and let me drive."

"What? No. I'm fine."

"You're not fine. Let me drive. I'll get you

there so you can see your dad for yourself. But you need to rest and calm down."

"Bossy," she said, finally giving in to the fatigue and apprehension clogging up her head.

Santo let her get in and then shut the passenger-side door. Then he came around and took over the wheel. "Rest," he said. "We'll get a bite to eat later."

"Not hungry," she replied. She wanted to pout and cry and have a fit but she had to be strong. Why hadn't Tilly mentioned any of this in all their daily calls? Why hadn't Ma told her that her daddy wasn't feeling well? Why had she left them all there alone to fend for themselves?

Why was she so glad that Santo was with her?

Why was she falling for him?

That was her last thought before she drifted off to sleep, her head shoved against the seat and caught against the window. When she woke with a gasp, she saw the exit sign for New Orleans up ahead. Her daddy was in a hospital there but Bayou Fontaine was only about twenty miles south of New Orleans and like that famous city, her hometown was centered around the Mississippi River.

A shard of homesickness hit her full force as they bypassed the sign to the right. "That's where I grew up," she said, her voice raw and husky. "Bayou Fontaine."

"You'll have to give me the tour one day."

"That wouldn't take long. Only one main street through town. River Drive."

"How are you?" he asked, his gaze touching on her.

"Better. I didn't realize how tired I was."

"We should be at the hospital in about fifteen minutes. Are you hungry?"

"No." She watched the traffic as they neared the city. "And Santo?"

"Hmm?"

"Thank you."

Chapter Sixteen

"Who is he?"

Davina turned from staring at the vending machine to find her older sister Alana's piercing deep blue eyes on her.

Not in the mood for a confrontation, she went blank. "Who is who?"

"That strange man you brought with you," Alana said, a hand tugging at her long dark hair. "Mr. Tall, Dark and Italian. I mean, he's good-looking but...kind of broody."

"He's a friend," Davina replied. "Santo. I introduced him to everyone but you were in with Da."

Alana's eyes brightened and then darkened. "Santo, as in Alvanetti?"

"Yes. My current client."

Alana actually smiled. "You brought a client home with you? And a nice-looking one at that."

"He's not staying," Davina retorted, her appetite gone. "He insisted on coming with me but he'll take a flight home now that I'm here. I told him I could drive by myself but my crew went all mutiny on me and kind of forced him into escorting me."

"Hmm. Interesting."

Davina shook her head and changed the subject. "What do you think, I mean, really think about Da?"

Alana's invisible nurse hat went on even though she was off duty tonight. "He's not taking care of himself. It's stress and worry and he doesn't eat right. You know Da loves his food but he needs to cut back and eat healthy. His blood pressure was off the charts when Ma called me this morning."

"She called you first?"

Alana nodded. "Yes. He didn't want any doctors. So I hurried over and I knew even before checking his vital signs that he needed to come to the hospital."

"Why didn't you call me immediately?"

"We called you when we had something to tell you," Alana said. "And I'm sorry I blamed you. It's nobody's fault. Da is who he is. Proud and stubborn."

"I should check in more, but Ma and Tilly

always assure me he's doing okay. Besides, he tells me to keep doing what I'm doing."

"It's okay," Alana said. "I was so upset and worried when I called, I took it out on you. I'm trying to do better about things like that. But…this is Da."

Relaxing a little bit, Davina nodded. "Those two traits—proud and stubborn, seem to run strong in our family."

"Tell me," Alana replied, her tone less confrontational now. "I was scared, Davina. I wanted you home."

"I'm here now," Davina said. And her eyes were wide open. She'd have to readjust her schedule to include more trips home.

Alana didn't speak but the sheen of tears in her eyes told Davina that her sister was still hurting from being jilted at the altar. Alana deserved better than that.

Davina thought back to Santo and Annette Pickett, the woman who'd verbally attacked him at the festival. How many people were walking around crushed and broken in this world, fear and hurt hidden behind their bitterness and anger?

She closed her eyes and said a prayer for everyone. For all of them. But mostly for her daddy.

When she looked up, Santo's gaze held hers.

Seeing him here, with her family all-around, brought her peace but also added to her angst. He didn't look out of place and that scared her because she wasn't ready for him to be in place yet. He'd talked to her brother Darren and they seemed to be getting along. He'd charmed Tilly and brought her coffee before she left to make a run home to check on things and bring back supplies for Ma. And she was pretty sure he'd win over Alana if her sister would quit being so standoffish. But she couldn't see Santo in her world on a permanent basis.

They were from different worlds.

They both came from big, confusing families and they both brought a lot of baggage with them but he was a widower with three children and she was a nomad who needed to keep moving. Santo was wealthy and settled into a routine with his children while she liked moving from one work site to the next. Could the two worlds merge?

She wasn't so sure. She shouldn't have let him come here with her. Everyone would jump to the wrong conclusion and assume too much. Her life would be one constant tease-fest.

Ma walked out of Da's room and reached out a hand. Davina took her mother's hand and then she hugged her close. "How is he?"

"Tired. But he's resting." Ma's green eyes

were misty with tears, her dark cropped hair haloing around her face. "They think he might have suffered a mild heart attack."

"I want to see him," Davina said.

"He'd like that," Ma replied. "He's been asking for you." She looked over Davina's shoulder. "For all of you." Then she lifted her head and said, "I want you to visit him but you are not to mention any of your worries or your observations or anything that you think has gone wrong in your lives. Your da carries the weight of the world for all of us. It's too much. We each have to share the responsibility of getting him well. Do I make myself clear?"

"Yes, Ma," Darren said, his reddish-brown shaggy mane hiding his solemn expression. He'd told Davina earlier that he and Da had been arguing when Da went pale and almost passed out.

The others echoed in agreement after their mother's stern warning.

Davina was about to go in, but Ma took her hand again and walked with her over to where Santo stood off to the side. "While you visit your daddy, Davina, I'll let Santo tell me all about the house you two are renovating."

Davina shot Santo an apologetic glance. "Of course, Ma. It's a real beauty."

"Go and see your father," Nancy Connell said, her tone serene. "I'll keep Santo company while you're gone."

Davina silently opened the door to her father's hospital room. She'd been in earlier but he'd been sleeping. Now he opened his eyes and smiled at her, his vivid blue eyes so like Darren's, his once thick reddish-brown hair now thinning and gray-streaked.

"Dani."

"It's me, Da."

"I must be pretty bad off for them to call you home."

"Not so bad. I just wanted to see you. You have some fancy machines hooked up to you so don't wiggle too much."

"Don't need machines. I'm fine. Just needed a little sleep."

"But you have to take care of yourself," she said, holding back tears. "I can come back and help Darren—"

"No."

The monitor beeped and the lines moving across it spiked.

"We'll talk about that later," she said, her own pulse quickening. "Just rest, okay?"

"You should get back to work, girl. So proud of you."

"Thank you, but aren't you proud of all of your children?"

"Of course. I tell 'em that all the time. Darren needs to find his place again."

"He will."

"Alana needs to love someone."

"I hope she can."

"Tilly…ah, my Tilly is such a joy."

"She's the best."

"Quinn isn't coming home, is he? 'Cause I'd know I'm bad off if you're bringing him home."

"No. We're keeping him posted. That is when we can get through to him. You know how that works."

"He's serving our country."

"Yes. My hero." Davina missed her younger brother Quinn so much, since they were close in age and they'd always had a special bond. Quinn would hug her and tell her it would be all better soon.

When her dad started drifting off again, she stood but he grabbed her hand. "Don't you worry about me, girl. You keep doing what you've been doing. I'm not blind, you know. You've been a good daughter, sneaking money to your ma."

Davina let out a sigh. "So does everyone know I've been doing that?"

"Of course. Can't keep a secret in this family."

He held her there, his smile softening as his medication kicked in and he drifted back to sleep. Davina held on until he was breathing peacefully and then she turned and left the room.

When she entered the waiting room, Santo stood and came to her. "How is he?"

"As aware and shrewd as ever," she said. "But he looks pale and tired. I think he's exhausted. Just completely exhausted."

"He's in a good place," Santo said. "The best doctors."

"Yes." She glanced around. "Tilly should have been back by now."

Her sister had gone home to get their mother a fresh change of clothes and some other necessities.

"You don't have to stay," she told Santo. "I'm with family now."

His expression filled with understanding and what looked like disappointment. "Of course. I'll grab a cab to the airport and catch a flight back to Florida."

"I shouldn't have let you do this," she said, her mind whirling with complications and concerns.

"I didn't mind," he said, his tone low. "You

got some rest on the way so that's a good thing, right?"

"Right."

"I can stay."

"No." She looked over at him, trying to find the strength to smile. "You go home and help my crew finish your house."

He took his time in responding, his eyes holding hers. "I guess that is for the best."

"I think so," she replied, wondering if this was some sort of ending to their budding relationship. Maybe he'd seen enough of her big family to decide he didn't want to be a part of it. Who could blame him? She'd sure seen enough to know she had no business longing for something she couldn't have right now.

She'd taken off on her own to prove herself but at what sacrifice to her family?

Santo's eyes held hers, so much unsaid between them. "I'll just go and tell your mother goodbye. She was really interested in the details of the house."

And other details, Davina was sure.

She watched as he shook hands and talked quietly to her mother. Then he came back to her. "I've called a taxi. I'll wait for it outside."

"Santo?"

"Yes?"

"I do appreciate you riding over here with me even if I did fall asleep on you."

"I liked watching you sleep," he said, his dark eyes centered on her. "I'll see you when you get back."

And with that, he was gone.

Davina stood against the cold hospital wall and watched him leave, her mind accepting that she was needed here more than she was needed back in Millbrook Lake.

She'd finish his house for him and then she would come home and take care of her family. No reason she couldn't work from Louisiana. She'd started out here and she could make a good living here.

But her heart wanted her to go out into the night and follow Santo home. Only her buzzing cell kept her from doing just that.

"Tilly, where are you?"

"Still at the house," Tilly said. "We've got a problem. The water heater is busted and the whole lower floor is flooded."

"I'm on my way," Davina said, ending the call.

"What's wrong?" Darren said, his head coming up.

Davina grimaced and motioned to him. "Busted water heater at home. Let's go."

Her brother didn't hesitate. "Ma, we'll be back as soon as we can."

Their mother nodded her head and held her hands together, a dejected expression on her face. "I'll be here."

Chapter Seventeen

Santo pulled his sedan up to the lake house and got out.

It was early. The sun peeked through the old oaks and towering pines across the lake in bold, creamy rays. The morning air was damp with dew and humidity, a frisky breeze awakening the fronds on the palm trees surrounding the house.

He stared at this new home and marveled at the changes taking place before his eyes. His heart had rearranged itself in the last few weeks. It had softened and stretched and… opened to the possibility of hope again. In some ways, he felt like this sunrise. New and fresh and warm. Almost happy again.

Now, standing here with this lemon-colored morning light shining on the bright white house with the new black shutters, Santo could imagine his children running across the gray-planked porch with the sky blue ceiling. He could see himself out on the lake in a sailboat, drifting, just drifting for the pure pleasure of it.

He could see Davina smiling and laughing with his children.

Whoa. That image stopped him in his tracks.

Did he dare hope? Did he give in to these new feelings that had him both excited and fearful?

"Are you gonna stand there all day?"

Santo whirled to find Rory and Blain staring at him from the curb. They'd obviously walked over to his house. "What are you two doing here?"

"We heard you might be in over your head," Blain said, grinning. "We came to rescue you."

Frowning, Santo shrugged. "I don't need rescuing."

"But you need to get this house finished, right?" Blain asked.

"Uh…yes, but—"

When Alec and Hunter showed up in Alec's fancy black truck, Santo wondered if this was an ambush or an intervention.

"What is going on?"

Hunter, who rarely spoke, explained. "We're gonna help you and the crew finish this house. So get over it and let's get it done."

Touched, even by such a blunt offering, Santo could only nod. "Davina will be happy."

"Well, we hope so," Rory said, chuckling. "Let's see if we can actually hammer nails and cut tile and then we'll see if she's happy."

"We have a crew, you know," Santo went on to say as they all walked toward the house.

"We heard," Blain said. "I called Kurt Martin and got the all-clear but we won't bother Davina with the details. He said Davina's blueprints and instructions leave little room for error. And besides, we'll only do basic stuff like buffing floors, laying carpet and changing out windows. Easy-peasy."

"Famous last words," Hunter said on an early-morning growl.

The rest of the crew came driving up and soon Kurt had all of them going at it. Santo had to stop every now and then and just watch the activity. Blain and his friends didn't have to be here on a beautiful Saturday morning. But friends did such things for people.

This house was becoming a real home.

And he was finally finding his way back to becoming a real father again.

He thought of Davina and wondered what she was doing and when she'd come back and for the first time in a long time, Santo said a prayer. For Davina and her family, for these men who showed him the example of forgiveness and friendship, and for himself and his children.

Then he went back to work.

Davina thought of the lake house.

Kurt had texted her and called her as needed over the last three days but it sounded like everything was on schedule there. Thankful that she was a little obsessive about having the best-laid plans on every project, she relaxed against the back of the waiting room chair and tried to make notes for Rikki on the interior of the house.

They'd need new furniture and artwork, a mixture of antiques and modern furnishings. Rikki could handle that part.

Davina hated missing out, hated not being there but she had to be here right now. She and Darren had declared the water heater as DOA, so that had been a new expense but they'd both paid half and now the old house by the river had immediate hot water. A luxury after years of hit-and-miss warm showers over the last decade or so.

They'd worked together seamlessly after picking up the new water heater early this morning, sometimes in silence and sometimes discussing what they should do next regarding their aging parents.

"Da isn't ready to throw in the towel," Darren told her. "But he can't keep this up much longer."

"I can come back and help," she offered. "We could try to work together, be partners."

Her brother gave her a long, measured stare. "Equal partners?"

"What else?"

"You created your own company and I've never seen a spot for me in that company," Darren replied.

"You resent me."

"Some, yeah," he admitted. "But I also admire you."

"And yet, you can't work with me?"

"I can't work *for* you. Dumb male pride."

"Stupid male pride. Do you and Alana think any of this has been easy for me?"

"No, we're aware of what you've done and what you've accomplished. But sibling rivalry is alive and well around here."

"Get over that," she suggested. "And when you do, call me and we'll figure out how to merge Da's company with mine, with you as my partner."

"I have one question," Darren said. "What made you strike out on your own anyway? You could have accomplished pretty much the same thing working with Da and me."

She finally told him the truth. "Da told me to do it. He thought he'd be holding me back. He knew I had a bad case of wanderlust so he suggested I start small and work my way up to creating my own company. And that's it. I went with his blessings but…I also went thinking he booted me out because I'm a woman. I never could tell any of you that."

"He's never once said that to me," Darren retorted, the old bitterness clear in his words. "I might not have been so tough on you if he'd explained it in that way. Or if you'd been honest with me."

"I didn't want to accuse Da," she said. "I could be wrong but I'm glad he sent me packing. I've learned a lot and I'm stronger for it."

"Does that make me stronger because you left then?"

"You could have done the same," she said, understanding his frustrations. "Would you have done it if he had given you his blessings and urged you to go?"

"I don't know," he admitted. "He always wanted me here to take over and yet, he won't let me take over. I stayed anyway, because I think I kept waiting—"

"For Lara?" Darren had been in love but it didn't work out.

"I don't know," he said again. "But I'm here and I'm not leaving. It's too late for me to leave."

"But you could be based here and still work with me."

He nodded, his eyes as dark as blue velvet. "I'll think about it…but not until Da is better."

They'd left it at that, but the more Davina thought about things, the more it made sense to partner up with Darren. He was as good at this as she was, since Da had trained them both.

Now if he could put his dumb male pride aside, they might get something going.

She glanced up when Tilly came out of Da's room.

"He's awake and feeling better," Tilly said, her grin sweet but not her usual perky full-blown one. "The doctor is going to update Ma when he makes rounds. And Nurse Alana the Hun is back on the case so she'll update us soon enough."

"You shouldn't call our sister names," Davina replied with a snort of laughter.

"You've seen her in action," Tilly whispered. "Makes Nurse Ratched look like a choir marm."

Alana walked out of their dad's room, her

blue scrubs clean and neat, her stethoscope slung around her neck in a precise curve, her wild curly hair caught up in a controlled chignon. When she cast a piercing look toward her sisters, Davina hid a giggle.

"Okay, I get it about the nickname," she said under her breath.

"Told you," Tilly said.

"What are you two mumbling about?" Alana asked after marching straight toward them in her bright pink floral orthopedic sneakers.

"Oh, this and that," Tilly said with a twisted grin. "How is Da? Tell us straight."

"His vitals are good," she said, suspicion still in her eyes. "We think he's had angina for weeks now but he didn't mention it to anyone. Just kept right on going." Glancing back, she lowered her voice. "Ma doesn't know the half of it yet. He's probably had a couple of mild heart attacks already. If we don't get this under control now, the next one could be fatal."

She went on explaining in medical terms but Davina followed enough to understand more tests were needed and he'd go home to a completely new lifestyle. More EKGs, more scans, more instructions. More medicine to avoid blood clots. He wouldn't be an invalid but he'd have to be careful and slowly build up his strength.

Knowing Da, this would not go over very well.

"Can he ever go back to work?" Tilly asked, tears in her eyes. "Because if he can't, he'll surely die."

Alana's stern expression changed as she sank down by her sister. Taking Tilly's hand in hers, she said, "Yes, he can go back to work. With stipulations. We have to get him on a proper diet and the right medications. Exercise is important, too. He works hard but that doesn't necessarily constitute the right kind of exertion to make him healthy."

"We'll all be here to make sure he does what he needs to do," Davina said.

"All of us?"

Alana's question hung in the air like a thin thread of twine.

"All of us," Davina replied without an explanation.

She still had to absorb what this could mean for her. All of her life, she'd only wanted to be away from Bayou Fontaine. Now she might wind up right back here. But what else could she do?

Her cell buzzed. Santo.

"Excuse me," she said to her curious sisters.

Then she got up and found the atrium overlooking a nice quiet courtyard around the corner. Staring out at the banana tree fronds and the elephant's ear plants, she spoke into the phone.

"Hi," he said. "How are you?"

"I'm okay." She gave him the latest update. "How are things there?"

"Steady." He told her what they'd accomplished in the three days since she'd been gone. "It's coming along. Today, we're retiling the new master bath."

"I hope you like how I redesigned it."

"I've always wanted a soaking tub."

"Ha. I put that in for future use."

"Future use?"

"In case you ever marry again...or sell to someone else. I also added that nice walk-in closet for more storage, too."

He went silent for a minute and then said, "You're always thinking ahead."

Was he upset that she had to consider every woman's dream—a big tub and a big closet?

"Part of my job but I can change it if you don't approve."

"I'm sure the kids will love the big tub."

"I hope so."

They talked about the house and her family

and how Virginia had hung strange artwork all over the room she'd taken at the bay house.

"It's eclectic and expensive artwork, at least," he said with a chuckle. "Nicely placed with an eye for detail. And the kids love it."

"They love her," Davina said, missing him and the kids and Virginia. "She probably made her room colorful and interesting so they'd be more comfortable with her."

"Then I guess we'd better consider that when we move."

"Done."

"I miss you," he said on what seemed like a final note.

"I miss you, too," she admitted, knowing it would have to do for now.

"When you get back, we need to talk."

Oh, mercy. They were going to do this in person with the-we-need-to-talk speech? She wasn't sure she could do that, not with Santo. "All right," she said, thinking this was not all right at all.

But it has to be done, she reminded herself. She'd never planned on getting a crush on her client. She'd never planned on that crush turning into something more.

When she hung up, her sisters were standing a few feet away, staring at her with such intensity she burst out laughing. "You both look ridiculous."

"We want to hear all about you and Santo," Tilly said without even flinching. "There's something brewing there. Even Ma noticed it."

"Ma thinks every man I meet has something brewing with me," Davina said, hoping that would shut them up.

It did not.

"Ma is very astute that way," Alana replied as they started back toward the waiting room. "I think Dani's finally met her match. And I think we will get the truth from her sooner or later."

"And I think you need your head examined," Davina retorted, squirming to get away.

"We'll get the details," Tilly announced with assurance. "All of them."

Another nurse walked up to them with a big white box. "Special delivery for Davina Connell."

"What is that?" Tilly asked, her eyes bright.

Davina saw the return address. "Marla's Marvelous Desserts. One of my favorite places in Millbrook Lake."

"Food?" Both of her sisters squealed like hungry piglets.

"Not just any food," Davina said, awe in her words. "Cupcakes. And the best in the world."

She tore open the shipping box and then the container to find a variety of her favorites from Chocolate-Pecan-Praline-Paradise to Lemon-Bar-None to Coconut-Crazy-Caramel and Really-Red-Velvet.

"I might cry," she said while nosy Alana read the card. "I can't thank Marla enough for sending this."

"Don't thank Marla," Alana said on a smug note. "Thank Mr. Santo Alvanetti. The very man you refuse to talk about." Poking Tilly to show her the card, she added, "And he signed it. 'Thinking of you and missing you.'"

Grabbing a cupcake, she said with a bright smile, "If he went to the trouble to send these and sign that card in that way, then you need to tell us more. Lots more."

Davina couldn't speak. Her heart filled with little torn pieces of joy. There was so much more going on than she wanted to tell right now. Mostly how she wasn't sure she'd ever be able to get over Santo Alvanetti.

Chapter Eighteen

Santo's palms were sweaty.

"I'm not so sure this is a good idea," he said for the tenth time.

Blain rolled his eyes.

Alec chuckled.

Rory said a prayer.

Hunter grunted.

"I don't think she'll like being surprised this way."

"Look, man," Hunter finally said. "You just need to go with this. Trust us. It works." He waved his hand in the air. "Every one of us brought a woman here…and every one of us married said woman."

Santo got up and went out on the big deck of AWOL, the camp house out on the bay where these four apparently sat around playing matchmaking games when they weren't fishing or hunting or watching the sports channel.

"Why did y'all target me?" he asked, uncomfortable under the intensity of their interrogating stares. "I'm not that guy. I'm not ready for a real relationship again." Then he hastily added, "No matter what you think about Davina and me."

"Right," Alec said. "Just keep telling yourself that."

Santo decided he had to make them understand. "Look, it's nice that you brought me out here for some R & R, but I don't belong here. I didn't serve my country the way all of you did."

"No, but we found a way around that," Rory explained. "You get in by default because Blain is now your brother-in-law."

"And because your family donated that million-dollar piece of jewelry to the Alexander and Vivian Caldwell Service Dog Association Training Facility, which brought in a lot of money at our silent auction last year," Alec added.

"And because you learned to say all of *that* without flubbing it the way I do," Hunter said on a droll note.

Rory slapped Santo on the back. "And because you're trying to make some changes in your life and you need a wingman or two or three."

Santo grabbed a soda out of the ice chest. "I've never had a lot of friends."

"We know," Blain said, grinning. "Don't worry. You'll get used to it."

"I need to thank all of you," he said, trying again. "The house looks great. When Davina gets back, we can finish up and I'll be able to move in."

"With her?"

"I don't know. We've only known each other a few weeks."

"Things happen fast around here, bro," Blain said.

"I need to take this slow," Santo replied. "You know what I've been through. I don't want to make another mistake."

Rory took a sip of his drink, his expression serious. "Davina is a good person, Santo. Nothing bad will happen if you fall in love again."

"Maybe not. But then, I didn't expect that the first time and look how that turned out."

Rory didn't speak for a couple of moments. "I can't promise things will be perfect...but sometimes when you see a second chance right there in front of you, you have to take a leap of faith and go for it."

"I don't know yet," he said, pacing back and

forth. "I want to take that next step with Davina but I'm not sure how."

"Like we said, you bring her here for a nice, romantic dinner," Alec said in his best sappy voice. When Santo balked again at their suggestion, he added, "Hey, don't blame us. Our wives thought up this plan."

"Based on?" Santo asked.

"Based on the way you and Davina seem to be skirting around the issue," Alec replied. "Who knows how women figure things out but they always do."

"It's a trap, man," Hunter said. "But it's a nice kind of trap."

Santo knew all of their stories. Fascinating stories of survival and faith and strength and danger and everything else you could throw in there. "What if I don't get that kind of ending," he said. "I don't know if Davina is ready for this. Ready for me."

"Well, since you're not so sure yourself maybe we shouldn't be pushing you," Rory said, giving him a clear out.

He turned to view the bay. It was late in the day and Davina would be home tomorrow. Home. No, not home. She'd be back here tomorrow to finish what she'd started. But they had to have that talk. The one where he told her he wasn't sure he could do this and he didn't expect anything from her. Or the one where she told him this had been nice but she had to keep moving on.

"I need some time to think," he admitted. "This is a great place. I never knew it was here."

"Most people don't," Alec said. "Just a couple of bad guys here and there but we took care of them."

"Is that a warning?" Santo asked with soft grin.

"If you hurt Davina, yeah," Blain said. "But it won't be us hunting you down. It'll be our wives. They all want her nearby for remodeling purposes."

"Oh, so they have an ulterior motive?"

"Of course." Rory laughed and flipped the juicy steaks he had on the grill. "The rule used to be—no girls allowed."

"Until we all broke it," Alec said.

"I didn't like that rule anyway," Blain retorted.

"I liked it and wanted to keep it," Hunter insisted. "But you know how that goes. I'll be glad when Chloe gets back from Oklahoma." He stood and put his hands in his jeans pockets. "Chloe and I made it against all the odds, man. You can, too."

Santo had met Hunter's wife, Chloe. She was

pretty and smart. They'd overcome a lot to be together and now Chloe was finishing up getting her PI license so they could work together to bring down corrupt people.

Santo turned and faced all of them. "You know, Davina and I don't have a history. Nothing to overcome except my background and her need to prove herself. I'm trapped in the shadow of my family's indiscretions and she doesn't want to settle down. Her company is growing. She needs to move on."

"Are you kidding me right now?" Hunter asked, giving Santo a firm eye roll.

"I'm serious."

"Excuses," Rory said. "Vanessa and I didn't have a history but we both sure had a past."

Santo gave up. "Okay, so I'd like to get to know Davina more and I'd like to keep her around. But that will have to be her decision and right now, it's not looking good. She might have to go back to Louisiana to help her family."

"It's not that far," Rory pointed out.

"No, it's not," Santo agreed. "But it's far enough."

"So what are you going to do?" Alec asked him.

Santo glanced around again. "I guess for

starters, I'm going to plan a romantic dinner here tomorrow night."

"Good plan," Alec said. "Marla's already got the cupcakes ready."

Santo thought it would take more than cupcakes to bring him and Davina together. But he couldn't let her go without trying to convince her to stay.

Davina parked her truck and stared up at the little apartment that had been her home for weeks now. Taking a deep breath, she checked her watch. Just enough time before dark to go by the lake house and check on things. She couldn't wait to see what Santo and the crew had done.

She stepped out of the truck and her cell rang.

Santo?

Did the man have a built-in radar that told him when she pulled into town?

"Hi," she said. "I just got back."

"I know. Rory called me."

"Well, that was thoughtful of him. Do you have people spying on me with some sort of coconut telegraph?"

"Yes. Stay right there. I'm coming to get you."

"But I'm tired and I need to freshen up. I want to go by the house."

"No, don't go by the house. Stay right there. Please?"

"Okay." She was too exhausted to argue. Maybe he was bringing one of Virginia's home-cooked meals. Her stomach jumped and rumbled at that since she hadn't eaten much since breakfast.

Davina checked her cell once again. No news from home.

She'd left reluctantly now that her dad had been home for a couple of days and situated into his new routine. He was doing great but she still worried about him.

"I could stay another week," she'd suggested this morning.

"I'll give you daily reports," Alana had promised her.

"I'll call you every night," Tilly said.

"I promise we'll let you know if he sneezes wrong," Ma had told her. "Now go and do your work. Your da wants you to do that. Knowing you're happy and back at work will do him good. He wants all of you to get on with your lives and stop treating him like an invalid."

"But I'm coming back, Ma," she'd insisted. "I'll be back as soon as I'm done with this project."

"Okay, honey," Ma had said with a secretive smile. "Okay."

So here she was, torn between duty and need. And so much more. Because finishing this house would be bittersweet on so many levels. It would be her first big job. And her last, until she could help Darren get Connell Construction up and running again. Maybe together, they could create the kind of homes that would put Connell Construction back on the map again.

She hurried and freshened up, combing her hair and putting on a clean blouse and jeans. When she heard a car outside, she was surprised to find a shiny blue pickup pulling up to her house.

A pickup driven by Santo and full of dark-haired children.

Davina couldn't stop the squeal that emitted from her lungs. Tears pierced her eyes.

"Oh, I've missed them so much," she said as she opened the door and rushed down the stairs.

So very much.

"Hello," she said, grabbing Nate up in her arms. "It's so good to see you."

"Dani," Nate said, poking at her shoulder with his chubby finger, his smile bright, his hair wild around his cute face.

"We made you things," Lucia said, her

hands widening to show big things. "But it's a surprise."

Adriana bobbed her head. "Miss Virginia baked all day and Miss Marla sent us cupcakes for dessert."

"I'm hungry," Davina admitted, her eyes catching on Santo. He looked even better than she remembered. Tanned, buff, less stressed, less fatigued. "So…let's eat?"

He moved close and took Nate and stood him down on the ground. "We're having a picnic," he explained. "But it's at a surprise location."

"Oh, okay. And to think, I almost put on my ball gown."

"You're silly," Adriana said, giggling as she took Davina's hand. "You can't wear a ball gown where we're going."

"I see you went shopping for a new car," Davina said once they were on their way, the children safe in the backseat of the big double-cabbed monster.

"Yes. Tearing down walls and renovating bathrooms made me feel manly."

He was already way too manly, she thought.

"I like it. Good for hauling things."

"We like it, too," Lucia said. "It's a truck but like a car. I feel safe in it."

"Like it, like it," Nate echoed.

"Where are we going?" she finally asked, too shocked and content to protest much.

Santo only smiled, his dark eyes full of something she recognized as hope. But she needed to tell him this couldn't be happening. She couldn't stay here.

Tomorrow or the day after, she thought. *Or a month or two from now. I'll tell him when the house is finally done.*

Santo pulled the big truck into a long and winding shell-covered road that seemed to lead to nowhere. She looked ahead and saw the bay shimmering beyond a big square house built high up on pilings.

"Where are we?" she asked, surprised yet again.

"We've gone AWOL," he said. "This is a special place where Alec, Blain, Rory and Hunter hang out a lot. It belongs to them but tonight we have it to ourselves."

Davina's heart tried to escape the joy and pain that merged like a great wave of water in the center of her soul and turned into a full-blown undertow. "Wow. I don't know what to say."

"You don't need to say anything," he told her. "Just for tonight, Davina, let's forget everything that's standing between us and enjoy being together."

She glanced from his hopeful face to the excited faces of his beautiful children. "I can do that," she said, her heart heavy with something so solid, she felt grounded for the first time in her life. "I'll be happy to do that."

So they all unloaded, baskets and boxes filled with surprises going with them to the front yard of the big house where the palmettos and magnolia trees and old oaks opened wide to the white sand of the bay.

"We're having a picnic," Santo told her again. "And then we're going to watch the sunset. I've heard it's really a good view of it from here."

"It's beautiful," she said, her gaze holding his.

She never wanted to leave. But she'd already promised her family back in Bayou Fontaine that she'd do just that.

Chapter Nineteen

The children frolicked and played in the water and got sprayed down with bug repellant and sunscreen several times. Virginia had thought of everything, Santo thought.

"Is it cupcake time yet?" Adriana asked, her dark eyes gleaming.

"Are you hungry already? You had two chicken legs," Davina said, grinning.

"Yes, and they were good but I want a cupcake," Adriana replied, her hand on her hip and her long hair falling loose from the once-neat ponytail she'd arrived with.

Santo went to the big basket they'd carted down to the beach. The sun was on its final stroll over the water and soon it would be full dark.

"Maybe we should let them eat dessert inside," Davina said. "The bugs are hungry, too."

"Good idea." He turned from the basket and whistled out toward the shallows. "Cupcakes inside."

"Why?" Lucia called, a sand bucket in her hand.

"Why?" Nate echoed from where he sat in the sand, making a crooked sandcastle.

"It's getting late," Santo explained. "C'mon now. We'll play inside games."

After they'd rounded up all three, the kids washed up and settled on a blanket in front of the massive television.

"Are we at a movie?" Nate asked, pointing.

"No, honey, we're in a man cave," Davina said, smiling over at Santo.

"Man cave, man cave," Nate chanted, giggling.

"I don't think children have ever entered these doors before," Santo told her as they fell in exhaustion onto the big, comfy man couch.

"How did you finagle this?" she asked, her heart content, her tummy full and her mind in turmoil.

"That's a funny story." Santo turned to her, his dark eyes solemn. "The guys brought me out here one night after I'd worked on the house. Actually, they helped with the house all weekend."

"The guys?" Davina knew which guys without even asking. She was just so surprised. "They joined you and the crew?"

"Yes and don't look so panicked. They were great. Even when we found the termites underneath the old master bathroom tub."

"Termites underneath the tub?"

"Yeah, a small colony. That delayed things for a couple of days."

"Yes, I know all about termites and what has to be done to get rid of them. I'm wondering why Kurt didn't call me about that."

"Because he didn't want to worry you and because I'm footing the bill and I was standing right there."

"That makes sense."

"I'm glad you see the logic. Anyway, the guys kind of forced me to come out here and then...told me that their wives think we should...continue in the same vein. You and me. Not them and me."

"You're cute when you're trying to explain something."

"I can't explain this," he said, a helpless look in his eyes. "I was told to come up with a romantic dinner but I panicked and brought the kids as a shield."

She let that admission soak in, knowing the truth was wrapped up in there somewhere.

"I'm glad you brought your children. I love your children. They need time with *you*. I don't mind spending time with *them*."

"And me?" he asked, a new vulnerability in his eyes. "Do you like spending time with me?"

"More than I want to admit," she said, giving him a sincere smile.

"So you don't want to spend time with me?"

"Yes, Santo. I enjoy being with you. And that's a big problem. I've broken my ironclad rule against becoming involved with a client."

"We can break some other rules," he said on a whisper. But he didn't touch her. His eyes said enough.

"I think one or two should be enough for now. As you said, let's forget everything else for a little while. I'm glad you brought the kids. I've missed all of you."

His gaze gentled as he glanced to his children and then back to her. "Well, that's all good and well, but I'm still not sure what's happening here."

"For tonight, we're having fun, right?"

"Right. Lots of fun."

"We can worry about the rest later," she said, deciding that was best for now. She had to stay here and finish the house and get him settled. Then…she'd go home.

But he didn't need to know the details. He'd probably already figured out the details. It didn't take much to see where this was headed.

"Okay, I agree," he said. "I'm pretty sure I suggested that all on my own. But Marla and those other very forceful wives and my interfering nanny came up with everything else."

"You mean even the artwork from the children?"

"Even that." They both peeked over at the framed drawings the kids had presented to her. The lake, shimmering in watercolor blues, from Lucia. The house, white and stark and with palm trees all around, created by Adriana. And a cupcake, bright and rich and definitely done in I'll-Miss-You-Chocolate from Nate.

"I love these masterpieces," she'd declared after they'd eaten grilled chicken and pasta salad and potato chips and peanut-butter-and-jelly sliders.

"Any other surprises?" she asked now, bracing herself. "Besides this place and cupcakes?"

"We found a snake at the lake house, living in one of the drainpipes."

"*No*, you didn't."

"He was tiny. A garden snake."

"I don't need details. Did you find him a good home?"

"Yes. Near the water. He has a great view now."

Santo leaned close. "I'd really like to kiss you right now."

Davina could go for that kiss. Right now.

"Cupcakes!"

Nate's loud squeal brought them apart.

"Hold that thought," she said, happy and relaxed for the first time in a week. "Let's eat dessert."

They shared a whole batch of Mala's latest culinary creations. Just-Kidding-Around-Creamy-Vanilla and Home-Is-Where-The-Heart-Is-Caramel-Apple.

"Marla is sending mixed signals," Davina pointed out, caramel icing on her finger.

"She thinks I might be doing that, too," Santo replied.

"Are you?"

"I think I am. It's confusing, being around you. One day, I'm all in with running away with you and the next, I'm back to being the stoic, angry man everyone tries to avoid."

She drew back to look at him. "Do you think *I'm* sending mixed signals?"

"I think you're trying to do what's right for yourself and your family."

"And so are you," she reminded him.

He gave her a soft smile and wiped the caramel off her cheek. "Somehow, we need to figure out a way to make things right for us."

Ready to get back to work, Davina rose early the next morning. The warm memories of last night stayed with her enough to ward off her fears and worries. If Santo was trying to win her over, he'd done a good job by bringing those children along as bait. How could anyone resent those three?

Santo could only work on the house a few more days and then he'd have to get back to work. She wanted to make the most of their time together. But she also wanted to reassure him that he could do this. He could be happy here with his children once she was gone.

"The boss is back," Kurt called, grabbing her to hug her tight.

"Thank goodness," Becky said, patting Davina on the head. "I kept 'em straight while you were gone, boss."

"Good. I've heard some tall tales, but I can't wait to see what you've done with the place."

After the others joined them and she gave them a full update on her dad, they all walked into the house and Davina stopped to take in the progress. The walls were back up, sturdy and painted a shimmering white called Sea Wind that had a hint of blue in it. The floors had been buffed and stained a rich burnished brown that highlighted the grain of the hand-scraped walnut. Covered with drop cloths while they worked, the new floors would be protected to the bitter end.

The dough box she'd found at a nearby antiques shop would have a place of prominence in the kitchen. Virginia had almost wept with joy when Davina had informed her of finding it.

"I can make bread from scratch," the nanny had declared, her expression dreamy. "Or at least pretend to, without actually having to use the dough box. Maybe we can use that for storage but I can sure use the surface for a lot of baking."

Virginia knew immediately that she'd found the family for her. Why couldn't Davina give in so easily to her feelings?

"The kitchen is coming along," Becky pointed out, her eyes gleaming with pride. "The new cabinets are perfect. Rikki worked hard with the builder to make them look old."

"They are exactly how I imagined," Davina said, moving her hand over the clean white wood and the ornate brass knobs and pulls on the cabinets and drawers. "The cornices add that extra richness. I'll have to send the cabinet builder a thank-you."

"Oh, he'll be thanked enough when you send him that big check," Kurt said with a deadpan expression.

The countertops were coming this week and she couldn't wait to run her hands over the white marble for the walled counters. They'd decided against marble for the island since the kids would use it for doing homework and helping with the cooking. There, they'd use a bacteria-and toxin-resistant bamboo to give a bit of pop to the center of the kitchen and to be more efficient and eco-friendly.

"It looks good," she said, wondering where Santo was. He'd told her he'd see her bright and early.

"We haven't made it upstairs yet," Kurt told her. "But the master bedroom is just about finished. We've primed it and now we'll go back and paint it that dreamy green you like so much."

"Distant Horizon," she said, remembering the names of every paint for every room.

"It's going to be so peaceful and welcoming," Becky said, a worried expression on her face. "Hey, boss, you okay?"

"I'm fine," Davina said. "Tired and still concerned about things back home."

"Well, everything here is okay and on track," Kurt replied. "You know you can count on us."

"I heard about the termites," she said, giving them a mock frown.

"And just who exactly told you about that?" Becky asked, her eyebrows lifting to meet her bangs.

"Santo," Davina admitted. "Since he had to pay for the treatments."

"Ah, Santo." Her crew members started teasing her.

"We think Santo has it bad for the boss," Josh said, walking by with a grin.

"We're friends," she retorted. If she said that enough maybe she'd believe it, too.

They got to work and things settled back into a routine.

But when Santo hadn't shown up at noon, she started to think maybe he wasn't as serious about this as she'd thought.

Finally, she got a text from him while she was nibbling on a pack of crackers.

Work emergency. Missing shipment. Sorry. I had to go to the office.

Davina went back to work, wishing she didn't miss Santo but glad for some breathing room while she got into the routine of work again. He was a distraction she shouldn't want around. But she did want him around. And that scared her.

But when she got a phone call later in the day from Virginia, Davina dropped her tools and informed her team she was leaving.

"Nate's in trouble," Virginia said. "He had an accident at preschool. Santo's with him. We're at the ER."

"I'll be there as soon as I can," she told Virginia before offering up a prayer. Santo had been with her when she'd gone to see her father. She'd be with him to see him through now.

That's what friends did for each other.

Chapter Twenty

"A broken wrist." Virginia shook her head. "But that's the nature of the thing. Kids go and go and then…something happens that you just didn't see coming."

"Do you know how it happened?" Davina asked, memories of broken bones and sprained ankles when she and siblings were growing up came back to the surface of her mind. "He's a pretty active little man."

"Tripped over a tree root walking in from the playground and fell right on his left wrist," Virginia explained. "It can happen so quickly."

"Are you sure he'll be okay?" Davina asked.

Virginia didn't speak. She seemed to be lost in her own thoughts. "Virginia?"

Virginia blinked and focused on Davina. "Oh, I'm sorry. What did you say?"

"You look tired," Davina said. "I can sit and wait until Santo comes out of the ER."

Santo was with Nate while they temporarily set his wrist to allow the swelling to go down. He'd have to have a small cast put on in a few days. Not easy for a boy his age.

"That might be a good idea. He told me to take the girls to his parents' house and leave them with the housekeeper because, of course, he can't leave Nathan. And I didn't want to leave either of them. I'll go pick up the girls in a little while."

Her eyes went blank again.

"Virginia, are you okay, really?"

"I'm fine," the older woman said. "I don't like hospitals."

Davina didn't pester the woman, but Virginia was usually the calm during the storm. Maybe Nate's accident had shaken her more than she wanted to let on.

Santo walked through the ER doors with Nate in his arms. The fresh tear streaks on Nate's face tore through Davina's heart. Nate saw her and burst into tears again.

"Dani."

She took him in her arms and kissed his forehead. "Hey, buddy. You had a bad day, huh?"

Nate gulped back tears. "Uh-huh." He touched his arm. "Off."

Santo let out a fatigued sigh. "He doesn't like his temporary cast."

"I don't blame him," Davina said. She glanced at Virginia. The woman had gone pale. Davina turned to Santo. "I can follow you two home while Virginia goes and picks up the girls."

Virginia snapped to. "Yes, good idea. I'll see you back at the house."

"She seems to be taking this hard," Davina told Santo as they walked out of the hospital together.

"I noticed that. She was certainly concerned when I called her. Insisted on coming here to be with us."

"She cares about all of you. We both do."

When they got to her car, she waited for Santo to take Nate. But the little boy refused to leave her arms.

"I'll ride with you," she told Santo. "We can get my car later."

They got Nate settled in his car seat and Davina got in beside him, her hand on his hurt arm. The trusting little boy kept his gaze on Davina until he started drifting off to sleep on the short ride home.

But Davina knew something for certain now.

She not only loved Santo's children. She was beginning to care about him in a big way, too.

* * *

The house was settled and quiet now.

Santo padded down the stairs in his socks, hoping no one would wake up again.

But he stopped at the bottom of the stairs and took his time looking at Davina. She sat in a chair she'd brought into the house to brighten things up. It had become the reading chair, as the kids loved to call it. She had her head against the broad, cushioned back, her eyes closed. Her hair fell in soft curls against the primary colors of the big floral chair.

She was beautiful and she looked right at home here.

He imagined her in the new house, puttering around the kitchen, straightening cushions, fussing over his children. She'd done all of those things and more tonight. Along with Virginia, she'd made sure his children were fed and bathed, done their homework and, finally, tucked into bed.

She'd kissed Nate good-night and told him she'd see him soon. Nate could see what Santo had been denying for weeks now, maybe from the very first day.

Santo's heart caught against a tangle of emotions.

He was falling in love with Davina.

"What are you doing?"

Santo whirled to find Virginia standing in the hallway underneath the open stairs in her bright red robe. "I don't know," he replied.

"Can I talk to you?" the nanny asked, her hands together in front of her in a tight grip.

"Yes." He came into the den and met her by the fireplace. "Would you like to talk in private?"

"No. I want Davina to hear this, too," Virginia said through a deep breath.

Davina sat up in the chair, her eyes bleary with sleep. "What's going on?"

Virginia marched over and sat down on an ottoman near Davina. "I need to make a confession."

Santo sank down on the couch. "I'm not so sure I *want* to hear this."

"No, you both need to listen and understand what I'm about to say."

Wide awake now, Davina leaned forward. "Go ahead," she told Virginia.

Virginia looked at Santo. "I love your children—"

"You're quitting?" he asked, panic in the question, his gut churning.

"No." Virginia held up her hand to shush him. "I don't want to quit. That's just it. I don't want you to fire me either."

"Then what is the problem?" he asked, his mind exploding with too many things at once.

"I need to tell you both where I came from," Virginia said.

"Oh, boy." Santo got up and paced the floor.

Davina reached out her hand. "Santo, sit down and let her explain."

He did, taking another breath, Davina's hand in his bringing on a calm he didn't feel. "Go ahead, Virginia."

"I was married once," Virginia said, her voice shaky. "It didn't go very well."

"You're divorced?" Davina asked, wishing she could help the poor woman. She'd never seen Virginia so afraid to speak.

"Yes. I left him after…after a terrible thing happened in our lives."

"What kind of thing?" Santo asked, his hand gripping Davina's. If somebody didn't explain soon, he was going to explode. No, no, he wasn't that man anymore. He took a deep breath. "Tell us, Virginia."

"I had two children."

Davina's gaze slammed into Santo's. "Okay," she said. "Go ahead."

"He took them from me," Virginia replied, her voice low now. "Took them right out from under me and tried to smuggle them away."

"You mean, kidnapped them?" Santo asked, his heart stopping.

"Yes. The divorce was ugly. He beat me a lot and I got custody of the children. He could only have supervised visits. So to punish me, he watched the house and I went inside just to get some snacks. They were playing in the yard where I could see them. But he got them when I turned away and took them. The police were chasing him and he had a horrible wreck. We lived in California then. So far away. He took my babies and me away from everyone."

Santo couldn't speak now. "Virginia, what happened?"

"They all died," she said on a long sob of a breath. "All gone in an instant."

Davina tried to stand but Virginia held up a hand. "Let me finish. I was a mess. Lost my job, almost lost my mind. Gave up on life. I had no one, no reason to live anymore. That was well over twenty-five years ago. But then about three years after it had happened, I heard in church about a course you could take to become a nanny. I thought after all the jobs I'd left or been fired from since I'd lost my babies, this one might work. So I sold my house and belongings and I went to England and I learned how to be a good nanny. It wasn't easy. I had this history, a past. But I didn't have a criminal record. And I passed all the necessary tests. But I never told anyone what I'd been through. I couldn't speak about it. I knew it would horrify people and I might not be able to work with children simply because people are afraid of grief and what it can do to a person."

Santo couldn't say a word. He looked at Davina for help. Virginia had hit on his personal fears and regrets in a way that jarred him.

"I'm so sorry, Virginia," Davina said. "I would have never thought—"

"No, no one would," Virginia explained. "I came back to the States and went into a panic. I lived in my car for two weeks because I was afraid to find work. But I finally saw an ad in the local paper. A single mom trying to make ends meet. I went for the interview and the poor woman was at her wit's end. I knew that feeling. I raised her little boy until he went to high school. Since then, I've roamed around and worked at two more homes, both good, solid homes." She stopped, gaining some of her old spunk. "Then I decided to come to Florida, to retire. I had relatives here. But my cousin showed me your ad and I called and talked to Rikki and, well, you know the rest." She gave Santo a steady glance. "You needed me and I hope you'll keep needing me, even if...if you get married again." Wiping at her eyes, she added, "You're all caught up now."

Santo shook his head. "We didn't know. Virginia, are you all right? I mean, I'm so sorry. Here you've helped me through a very bad time and...you're still grieving."

"We never stop grieving," Virginia said, her tone firm and clear. "But I'm okay. Your children are safe with me. I hope you'll let me stay with them until they go off to high school, too."

"Of course," Santo said. "I wouldn't have it any other way."

Davina finally stood and went to Virginia. Falling on her knees, she touched her hands to Virginia's arms. "When Nate got hurt, you had a flashback of all that happened, right?"

Virginia nodded, tears forming in her eyes. "The school called me and I hurried right away. When I walked into the ER, it all came rushing back. I'm sorry. I can usually handle this type of situation but...this was little Nate. He's the youngest I've ever taken care of and he's a year younger than my daughter. I had a daughter who was three and my son was seven. Janie and Frederick. I kept remembering them all day. I didn't want to scare either of you, but I had to tell you. In case I had a nightmare like I used to. I didn't want to upset the children or make you think I was some sort of weird nanny."

Davina hugged Virginia close. "I'm so glad you're here and that you told us this. I'll feel better when I'm gone, knowing you'll take care of Santo and his children."

Virginia searched Santo's face. The look she gave him begged him to do what needed to be done. She didn't want Davina to leave either, but Davina had just announced she'd be doing that very thing, no matter what.

Santo took Davina to get her car, his mind reeling with the acceptance of what she'd said to Virginia. He'd have to let her go. She wasn't the kind to do this even if she did have a way of soothing him and his children. Davina had a whole bright future ahead of her. He'd already had one bad marriage, which made his future shaky in the love department. But he couldn't blame its failure completely on his misguided, sick wife. He'd neglected his marriage because of work and he'd almost done the same thing with his children.

He wouldn't risk putting Davina through that and he couldn't risk falling for her while she was so wrapped up in her own career and her family's needs. He had to let her go.

"Thank you for helping out tonight," he said.

"Sometimes I feel inadequate as a dad and I think I should be able to handle things on my own. But it's not easy."

She settled against the seat and let out a sigh. "No, it's not. I have experience since I have such a large family. Our parents taught us to pitch in, to help out as needed and to dive in with both feet. I sometimes overstep in that area."

"I like the way you overstep," he said when they'd reached her car. He turned off the truck's engine and turned to her. "Can you believe what Virginia must have gone through?"

"More than a person should have to endure but it explains how cryptic she's been about her past at times. No wonder she seemed so distant and pale today."

"I think she's afraid I'll fire her."

"Promise me you won't."

"I promise."

"I guess I should get going. Don't worry about coming to work at the lake house tomorrow. Nate will want his daddy."

"I'll see how things go," he told her, wishing he could say more. "Maybe I'll ride over later and see how far you and the crew have advanced."

"Okay." She touched her hand to his. "Get some rest."

Santo stared into her eyes and then against his better judgement, he tugged her close and kissed her. Then he sat back. "You, too."

Davina's eyes darkened and glistened underneath the parking lot security lights. "Good night."

Then she got out of the truck and hurried to her own.

Santo sat there with his hands on the steering wheel, watching until her vehicle disappeared into the night.

Chapter Twenty-One

The next few weeks moved at a rapid pace. Davina and the crew worked from early morning to sundown, going from room to room and remodeling. New walls and windows, shiny new floors and carpet, updated cabinets and closet space and a clean crisp freshness all over the house, all of these occupied her time.

Santo occupied her mind, however.

He'd pulled away after Nate's accident. He worked with the crew here and there, but he spent the last few days of his time off with his children. Davina and he still talked and laughed and she hung out with the kids when she had down time. But Virginia was usually the one there. Not Santo.

He worked all day and devoted his spare time to his family. He brought the children to the lake house at times, to let them see the updates and to show them their rooms. He'd helped out on the weekends for a few hours, but he avoided Davina and concentrated on following Kurt's orders.

"I can't wait to move in here," Lucia told Davina just yesterday. "This is the best new house ever." She skipped to one of the big windows. "Daddy's gonna put up a swing on that big oak tree. He said."

"I'm sure he'll do just that," Davina replied. "I'll be glad to help him."

The bay house had several showings and according to Rikki seemed to be on several buyers' radars.

"I think by the time school ends, we'll have a buyer," she told Davina.

Tonight, Davina came home to her little apartment and took a long shower. It had been a warm day and they'd all worked up a sticky sweat, the humidity feeling like glue against their clothes and skin. Santo hadn't come by, but he'd called her to get a status check.

"We have some buyers who are coming back for a second look," he said.

"Maybe they'll be the ones."

She hadn't heard back from him. They seemed to be at an impasse. A place where they'd both decided to get through this and move on. A place where they'd just ignore their feelings for each other. Davina didn't like that place.

She'd just put on black leggings and a white linen tunic and was about to call and check on her dad when her doorbell rang. Surprised, Davina squinted into the peephole.

Rikki stood there, her dark hair pulled up in a loose bun.

Davina opened the door and smiled. "Hi, what brings you by tonight?"

Rikki pushed her way in and motioned behind her. "We came to rescue you."

Davina looked beyond Rikki to find Marla, Vanessa and Chloe marching up the planked steps to the tiny porch, all dressed as casual as she was. "What's going on?"

"Spa night," Marla declared, holding a basket that held all kinds of creams, lotions and polish. Along with some serious primping equipment.

"I don't recall asking for a spa night," Davina said, her mouth falling open when Chloe, all girl-next-door fresh and looking chic as always in a floral tunic and bright leggings, her tawny hair down around her shoulders, carried in bags of good-smelling food.

"It's a surprise," Vanessa said, laughing. She held drinks and what looked like dessert. "You've been working hard and since you're all alone here and your family has been dealing with a lot, we decided we'd do a girls' night in."

"Yes," Marla said. "We wanted to hold this fun-fest at AWOL, but the guys are all there and for now, they've reestablished the no-girls-allowed policy."

"They confiscated my stubborn brother," Rikki said. "Santo needs a break, too. He's been working hard but he's spent more time with the girls and Nate lately, so even he needs some downtime."

Vanessa dumped her packages on the counter. "Besides, he has a lot to celebrate."

"Why is that?" Davina asked in a controlled voice.

"The house sold today," Rikki said. "Didn't he call you?"

Davina's stomach knotted. "No, he told me he had some serious return lookers but when I didn't hear from him, I thought maybe nothing happened." She watched as Marla and Chloe unloaded all the loot. "That means he'll need to move soon, right? I'll have to speed up things on the lake house."

"He has a month," Rikki told her, understanding in her eyes. "Meantime, we'll hold a garage sale and start packing up what little he'll be keeping."

"This is really happening," Davina muttered,

both happy and sad. "He'll finally get to start his new life."

The other four women stood around the tiny counter and stared over at her.

"We all hope you'll be a part of that life," Marla said.

Davina shook her head. "I don't think so."

Rikki put a hand on the counter. "Do you want to be with Santo?"

"I...I don't know. He's become so distant lately. I think he has to decide if he's ready to have another woman in his life."

"He's trying to do the right thing," Rikki said. "He knows you want to go back to Bayou Fontaine to be with your family. I think he's afraid of holding you back." She sighed. "And my brother still has a bad case of cold feet in the relationship department. Be patient with him, okay?"

"I am patient," Davina admitted. "I can tell he's not ready to make any type of commitment and I've accepted that, but then I'm not so sure about our relationship either. You're right. I do need to go home and I can't predict what will happen when I get there."

"It's not that far," Vanessa said. "Rory and I managed a long-distance relationship when I still lived in New Orleans and we made it through while I came back and forth before the wedding."

"But you two knew you were in love," Davina said. She'd heard their story and it hadn't been easy.

"I fought it," Vanessa said. "Fought against loving him and now I can't imagine my life with anyone else."

Davina couldn't imagine her life without Santo and his children in it but how was she supposed to be in two places at once? Those kids needed stability, not someone who came and went in their lives. And she'd have to do that until her family was solid again and her dad's health was better.

"What's going on between you two?" Marla asked as they spread out the food. Chicken salad and crackers, cheese and fruit.

"Have you ever noticed that we eat all the time?" Davina asked to stall the questions.

"Yes, now tell us how you feel," Chloe said with a soft grin. "We didn't just come here for manicures. We want the scoop on the most talked-about couple in town."

"Are people gossiping?" Davina asked, not surprised.

"Oh, people always talk," Marla said, a carrot in her hand. "Annette Pickett seems to be spreading rumors and even letting people who look at the bay house know what went on there. That woman is a piece of work."

"I thought Rory had talked to her," Davina said.

"He has talked to her and he mentioned Santo's job offer but she said it was insulting so she refuses to meet with Santo to discuss anything. She's bitter and that's understandable but…it's affecting her children, too."

Davina dipped a carrot into some hummus. "Maybe that's why Santo's cooled his jets. He's protecting his children."

"And he's shielding you from that kind of unfortunate stuff," Chloe said. "But all that aside, talk to us. We only gossip about the good stuff."

Davina smiled at that. "I feel as if I've found an old wall and discovered a treasure hidden behind it," Davina said. "I've torn down walls all my life but Santo has been a challenge. He's strong and unwilling to bend at times, but at other times he's tender and sweet. I can't decide what he's thinking."

"Keep tearing away," Rikki said, between bites of fresh Alabama strawberries. "My brother needs someone good in his life. And besides, his kids adore you."

Touched that they all liked her enough to

cheer her on, Davina wasn't so sure Santo was ready or willing to make the next move.

"There is a lot to consider," she said.

"Okay, enough," Marla ordered. "It's time for facials and pedicures and polished nails." Pointing to the dessert bag, she said, "And praline cheesecake."

"Can we just skip to the cheesecake?" Chloe asked.

"Spa and then dessert."

"You're tough," Vanessa told Marla.

"I hope our men will be just as tough on Santo," Marla quipped. "Somebody needs to talk some sense into that man."

They all laughed and soon, they had Davina in a chair with her feet soaking in lavender oil and wonderfully hot water and her nails glowing with a light pink polish that Rikki called "Pinky Power."

"You know I'll ruin these first thing tomorrow, don't you?" Davina asked.

"Enjoy them tonight then," Marla suggested.

They took turns doing each other's nails, giving each other neck massages and laughing as they plastered smelly masks on their faces and took selfies.

The night went on and Davina relaxed and had a good time. They ate cheesecake, danced like schoolgirls and laughed while they discussed the men in their lives.

When the clock struck midnight, Marla announced it was time to go but Davina knew she'd made friends for life. "I haven't done this in a long time," she admitted. "My sisters and I used to be so close and now we're all caught up in our own lives and just trying to stay afloat. Thank you for coming to see me."

"We had fun," Marla said. "We love our men but, hey, every woman needs some girl time, right?"

"Right," came the echo as they cleaned up and left, hugging and laughing and promising they'd do it all again soon.

Davina's apartment went silent again.

Then her cell rang.

"Da's back in the hospital," Tilly said, her voice shaky. "I think you need to get home as soon as you can."

Sleepy and still wondering why his four new friends had come close to throttling him because he hadn't made any progress with Davina, Santo walked through the warehouse the next morning in a dour mood. That mood only got worse when he had to go over shipment orders and send out emails demanding answers for problem areas. The Alvanetti Imports store had been open for six months now and they were finally beginning to see a small profit, but lost orders and damaged goods were always a problem.

He really did need an assistant. Someone who could shadow him and get things done. His secretary was great at making his daily schedule bearable but she didn't know the ins and outs of running a wholesale commercial business.

Santo thought about Annette Pickett. She'd refused to consider his job offer. Rory had talked to her, urged her to reconsider and meet with Santo, but she wouldn't bulge. She didn't want any part of the Alvanetti family.

Why? Pulling out his phone, Santo found the number Rory had given him. Annette Pickett's number. Did he dare call the woman?

The Alvanetti name was becoming synonymous with high quality furnishings and a lot of the builders were using them exclusively. That meant big volume shipments for the continuous stream of condos and luxury homes that were going up all across the state. So business could only increase over the next few years. He had to show the world that this was a solid, by-the-book, legal operation.

His sister had certainly utilized the family

store in both of his houses. Now the bay house was sold. He'd be able to move into the lake house in a few weeks.

Davina.

He hadn't called her about the house selling and he wasn't going to have time to go by and see her today. After talking to one of his warehouse foremen about some broken vases that had been shipped from Italy, he headed back to the office to call Davina. He owed her that news at least. As for the rest, he'd pointedly told his buddies to back off. This was between him and Davina.

That hadn't fazed them, of course. They wanted an update later in the week. He'd better call Davina or she'd hear all kinds of things from their bossy wives, too.

But his cell rang before he could make the call.

"Rikki? Hi."

"Hi," his sister said. "Listen, Davina had to go to New Orleans. Her father is back in the hospital and it's not looking good."

"Really?" She hadn't called him. "When did this happen?"

"Late last night after we'd left her house. She got dressed and took off as soon as she heard. Drove all night to get there, from what Rory told me."

Santo held two fingers between his eyes and rubbed the throbbing beat there. "So this is bad?"

"Yes. He had a massive heart attack. They don't think he's going to make it."

"Can you help Virginia with the kids?"

"Of course. Go."

Santo didn't waste any time. He called in his top people, explained the situation and then called Virginia. "I'll be home to give the kids a kiss and grab some clothes. Will you be okay with them for a few days?"

"Of course. Give Davina my love."

He was on his way to New Orleans an hour later.

Chapter Twenty-Two

Davina stood huddled with her sisters.

Ma stood with Darren by their daddy's bed.

The room was cold but she shook mostly because she couldn't believe her sweet, hard-working daddy wasn't going to make it.

"This can't be real," she said, wishing she'd stayed here over the last couple of weeks. "I thought he was better."

"He tried to get better but…he's so tired," Tilly said, her hand on Davina's arm. "This one just hit him out of the blue. And in his sleep at that."

Alana wiped at her eyes. "He's only alive because of sheer grit. Just be prepared. He could go to sleep and not wake up."

"Is Quinn coming home?" Davina asked, praying her brother would be able to make it in time.

"We're still trying to reach him."

Ma motioned to her. "He wants to speak to you, Dani."

He was speaking to his children, one by one.

Dani didn't want to have this talk. Not at all.

Ma never called her by her nickname. She wouldn't break down. Not now, when Da was trying to tell them goodbye. Wondering what he'd said to Darren, she glanced at her brother's stoic face. But Darren didn't even look at Davina. He marched out into the waiting room without a word.

Alana and Tilly held on to each other, knowing their turn was coming. She wished Quinn were here.

Davina went to her daddy and took his hand. He opened his eyes wide and gave her a weak smile. "Did good."

She knew what he was trying to say but she didn't care right now. "Why did you send me away? I could have helped right here."

"Did help. Did fine."

"I should have stayed. I'm not leaving Ma again."

"Shhh. Live your life. Live, you hear."

"I can't, Da. Not without you here."

"Yes, you can. Strongest of all."

She shook her head and kissed him. "Rest. I love you."

"I love you, my good girl. Keep at it but find some love out there, okay."

Davina thought about Santo. "I will, Da. I promise."

Then he motioned. "Alana."

Davina reluctantly let go of his hand and turned toward her sister. "Alana."

Alana gulped a sob as she walked by their mother. Davina moved away and went into her mother's arms. "We have to do something."

Nancy looked into her eyes. "It's not ours to fix, honey. He's going home to God."

"I don't want God to have him."

"Of course you don't. But your da is ready and he'll be all fresh and new when he gets there."

Davina wiped at her eyes and pulled away. She needed some air. Tilly hovered in the corner, afraid. Davina wanted to run away from this room and this hospital but she had to be strong for Tilly. She could see it now. She'd always been strong and determined and impulsive and independent. Caught in the middle, she'd been torn between all of them. Da had seen it—the stifling of her creativity, with everyone around her telling her what to do and how to act. With her trying to take care of everyone and failing.

He'd needed Darren to stay. So he'd sent her away.

Alana passed her, crying. Tilly shook her head. "I can't do this."

"Yes, you can," Ma said, urging her forward. "You'll do this for him, understand?"

Tilly bent her head and hurried to their daddy's bedside, bobbing her head as he looked up at her with those vivid dark blue eyes.

After Tilly came back, they both went outside.

"He's waiting for Quinn to get here," Tilly said through her tears. "He'll hold out till that."

Davina knew that was true. Quinn would want to be here in Da's last hours.

She held on to Tilly, comforting her little sister while her own heart shattered like chipped tile pieces all around her. Tilly's head came up and she gasped, causing Davina to whirl to see if Quinn was finally here.

But her baby brother wasn't standing there by the wide door to the cardiac care unit.

Santo was. He took one look at her and held out his arms.

Davina went straight into his warm embrace and held him close, her tears misting against his crisp white shirt.

She never wanted to let go.

* * *

"What are you doing here?" she asked later when she could breathe again.

"I came as soon as I heard," Santo said. "You can't go through this alone."

Wiping at her eyes, she said, "I'm not alone but I have to admit seeing you standing there made me feel a whole lot better."

All around them, friends and relatives were talking quietly. Dawn was popping up outside in muted pinks and yellows that looked like cotton candy floating over the trees and buildings. Davina's bones were so weary that she thought she'd collapse if she tried to stand.

"It's been a long night," she said. "We're waiting for Quinn. He tried to get leave when we finally got word to him that Da had the first heart attack but we don't know if he's on his way or if he'll make it."

Santo listened and held her hand, his gaze on her. "Is there any hope?"

She shook her head. "Surgery would kill him and there's nothing else they can do at this point. Alana says he has coronary heart disease and no one caught it in time, mainly because he refused to go to a doctor. I want to be so mad at him for that, but I can't. I just can't."

"I'm so sorry." His fingers tightened on hers.

"Rory and Vanessa are coming later. I'm sure they'll be a comfort to you."

"They don't have to do that."

"They want to do that," he replied. "You have new friends now, Davina. We'll help you get through this."

She couldn't speak. Thoughts of Millbrook Lake and his beautiful house went to the back of her mind. All she could think about was how she'd abandoned her family. She should have put her foot down and explained to her parents that she needed to stay. They all needed to stay. Even Alana, who still lived and worked in New Orleans, had pulled away from them in the last few years and now guilt was eating at her, too. Darren had stayed but he'd resented every minute of it. And Tilly just wanted everyone to be happy, but how could she make that happen now?

Santo came because he knew all about that gnawing, all-consuming kind of guilt.

"You don't have to stay," she kept telling him.

"I'm not leaving you," he replied. "I didn't have a whole lot of people on my side when Althea…died. It was a horrible time. Blain couldn't even look at me because he had to shoot my wife in order to save Rikki. He wouldn't leave Rikki's side either. We almost lost her so I don't blame him for watching over her even after the case had been solved. And I wonder sometimes, if things had gone the other way and if Rikki had been killed, how would I have felt about Althea then? How would my children cope with that? It was just a horrible time and…I think that's why I've held back on…everything."

On them. He didn't have to say the words to tell Davina why he'd been avoiding her lately. They'd grown too close for comfort because they'd both been through so many things that had shaped them and molded them.

"Did you feel torn?" she asked, needing to understand.

He nodded. "In about fifty different directions. Torn between my loyalty to my father and my siblings and torn between the truth and the lies. Torn because my children lost their mother and destroyed because I couldn't explain why. I hated myself because I was so blind, so clueless, that my own wife tricked my entire family right underneath my nose. I don't know if I'll ever recover but…I'm trying."

"Santo, I'm so sorry. Losing my daddy is going to be the hardest thing in my life but what you've been through is the worst."

He shook his head, tears in his eyes. "When you lose a loved one, good or bad, close or not so close, it's always hard to deal with. My mother has such a strong faith. She told me that we're only on this earth a short time. She wants me to embrace life while I'm still here. And you've helped me to do that."

Davina didn't know what to say. So she said the only thing she could. "Thank you for coming. It means the world to me."

Before Santo could reply, Tilly came rushing up to her.

"Quinn's on his way. He was already on his way before this happened, thankfully. He should be here by nightfall."

Davina hugged her sister close. "That's good news."

Santo stood to the side and out of their way but her eyes met his over Tilly's shoulder. She couldn't explain how much having him here meant to her. And she couldn't explain how much it meant that he'd shared some of his own pain with her.

They might not be able to come to terms on being together but she knew one thing for sure. Santo would always have a place in her heart and he'd be her friend for life.

She might have to accept that as her only comfort for now and thank God for the blessing of having Santo as a friend.

Chapter Twenty-Three

"Shhh. She's coming."

Santo held his hand up to all the people he'd smuggled into his new home, signaling that Davina had arrived. This impromptu house-warming party had been the brainchild of his sister and her well-meaning friends, but he hoped Davina wouldn't take it the wrong way.

It had been a month since her father died and she'd been back and forth between finishing this house and doing what she could to help her family. Each time she left, he lost a little bit of her. Davina had promised to come back one last time, to see him and the children finally in the house with everything in place. One last evening together.

Then, she'd be out of his life forever.

"Unless we throw a big party and show her how much we want her to stay," Rikki had suggested. "We can do it over Memorial Day weekend."

Now Santo wished he'd stuck to his original plan and kept things low-key, just the two of them and the children.

Too late for that. She was standing on the curb, looking up at the house with awe in her eyes and a soft smile on her pretty face. She looked small, her features hollowed out. She'd lost weight. But she was still beautiful. Her long floral dress wrapped against her calves in soft folds, the wind lifting it out like flowers on a breeze. Her hair fell around her cheeks in a rustle of reds and coppers. It was hard to read her expression but she looked sad and afraid, a distant longing settling over her features.

He almost went to her.

"Here she comes," Rikki said, excitement in her voice.

Davina had helped his sister to heal, too.

Okay, Lord, help me make this right. I'm in love with this woman but I'm so afraid of telling her how I feel.

He hoped his feeble prayer had been heard. Rory always said the Lord heard prayers even when you didn't know you were praying them.

The children started squirming and giggling when the doorbell rang. "Shhh," he said with a grin.

Then he opened the door. "Hi. It's good to see you."

She stared at him and then looked inside. "Why is it so dark in there? I know I put lights in the best places to show off the—"

He pulled her inside and hugged her close. "I'm sorry for this but—"

"Surprise!"

About twenty adults and three very eager children came rushing at them. He held Davina back and gave her an apologetic gaze. "It wasn't my idea."

She stared up at him, blinked away tears, and then peeked over his shoulder at the room full of people waiting for her.

And then she turned and ran back down the front steps.

"Dani!"

Not even Nate calling after her could make Davina go back inside that house. Tears flowing down her face, she kept walking until she was out of breath. When she looked up, she was at the church. She almost went inside the apartment that she'd come here to shut down for good. But instead she walked into the small prayer garden Rory had been working on all spring.

Davina sank down on a Monet bench made

out of eucalyptus wood that he'd ordered on her recommendation. She touched her fingers to the beautiful golden-brown grain. Why did she always feel so safe around old wood?

The wind off the lake tickled at the fan palms centered on one side of the tiny rectangular garden and frolicked over the chimes Vanessa had hung on a crape myrtle tree. The smell of gardenias and jasmine lifted into the dewy early evening air. Somewhere off in the distance, a child's laughter floated through the trees and a dog barked a playful, frisky answer. Somewhere, the smell of wood smoke indicated that someone was cooking on a grill.

Davina closed her eyes and thanked God for bringing her to this small, quaint little town. She'd never forget her time here. While she'd stayed busy and her personal life had changed dramatically, this place had given her a sense of peace.

"I wish you could see this, Da," she whispered on the wind. "That house is so amazing. They'll be so happy there. I promise I'm going to make our house that special again one day. For you."

When she opened her eyes, Santo was standing underneath the jasmine-covered pergola, his hands in the pockets of his jeans.

Wiping at her eyes, she croaked, "Did you hear all of that?"

"Yes," he said. "And you're right. He would be proud."

She smiled and let out a sob of a breath. "I wish I could stay, Santo."

"I'm so sorry," he said, moving closer, hesitating. "I tried to tell them you might not be ready…"

"It's not that," she said, wiping at her eyes. "It's not that at all. Seeing everyone there just took me by surprise because you've all been so welcoming to me and…this just added to that. I didn't mean to be so rude."

"They understand. I told them to stay put so I could talk to you in private. But with one call, they'll all be gone if you don't want to see them."

"That's the problem," she said, motioning for him to join her on the bench. "I do want to see them. But I'm such a mess these days. My crew was there, right?"

He nodded. "They came back to surprise you. And spend some time on the water during Memorial Day, of course."

She laughed at that. "Yes, I think Kurt has developed a strong fishing addiction."

"Nothing wrong with that. I think the AWOL crowd is going to do some deep-sea fishing next weekend. I've never had good friends before. I don't know why I waited so long."

"They are good friends," she said. "I'll miss all of you."

"So…you're leaving us?"

"I don't see any other way. Darren is taking over the company but he needs my help. Ma wants to move out of the house but Darren is going to move in with her and try to fix it up. And Tilly's living there for now." She shrugged. "I want to help with that. My mother deserves a nice place to spend the rest of her years."

"Yes, she does. How's she doing?"

"She's strong and her faith is solid, but we find her crying alone in the little sitting room, where they always watched television together. One chair is always empty now and none of us can bring ourselves to sit in it."

Santo put an arm around her and tugged her close. "I know that kind of emptiness. Even after everything Althea did, I would still look up expecting to see her coming down the stairs." Taking a deep sigh, he added, "But you know what? Now, in the lake house, I look expecting to see someone else coming toward me."

Davina started crying all over again. "Me?"

"No," he said to make her laugh. "Becky. I've got this crush on her."

Davina slapped at his arm. "Right."

"Of course you, always you," he said. "I won't force you to make a choice since I've learned lately about the importance of family. But I want you to know something."

"What's that?"

"I will be here, waiting for you to come back to me."

"But I—"

"I mean it," he said. "I love you. I fell for you the day you walked into my house wearing that cute tool belt. When you took my son into your arms and comforted him, my heart began to heal. You have to come back to me, okay?"

"I can't promise—"

"Try."

"I'll try," she said. "It's just all so confusing right now."

"I'm willing to give you some time."

"Okay."

"And we can visit now and then, right?"

"Right."

"You don't seem so sure."

"I don't know what's going to happen. All I know is work."

"You should remember what that'll get you."

"I do. But for the next few months at least."

Santo felt her slipping away again. "I love you," he said. Then he kissed her to show her he was ready. She kissed him back and smiled up at him but he could see it in her eyes.

She'd already made her decision. She hadn't told him that she loved him, too.

Then she surprised him. "I'm starving. I think I'm ready to go back to the house now. I want to see the children. So I'll have some good memories to take with me."

A month later, Davina and her brother Darren were busy in what they'd turned into a downstairs bed and bath in her parents' house. They were giving their mom her own apartment, downstairs near the kitchen but with a sitting room and galley-style kitchen on one wall and a nice bedroom with a private bath. A camera crew was following them around. Just a local team from the evening news that wanted to highlight remodeling older homes in Bayou Fontaine. Tilly had sent in a picture of Santo's lake house, citing Davina's skills.

Things were turning around but she couldn't leave until she and Darren had an ironclad agreement regarding the company, starting with getting this house completely overhauled.

Santo called her a lot. They talked about getting together but just as she knew would happen, they were both too busy. The Fourth of

July was coming up. He wanted her to come to Millbrook Lake for the weekend.

But she wasn't sure that could happen.

Finally, Ma came into the big bedroom, her eyes glistening with pride. "Your Da would think we were living in the Garden District," she stated, tears forming. "I don't deserve such luxury."

"Yes, you do," both Davina and Darren said.

They were equal partners now. Working together, they'd discovered all kinds of ways to streamline the business and make things more efficient.

"You don't have to be here 24/7," he told her while their mother listened and nodded. "We've got a system now. You can do the regional work and I'll hold down the local construction projects. We're well-known thanks to your latest remodel down in Florida."

"I'll say," Ma added. "A film crew and talk of a reality show."

"I'm not doing a reality show unless it's all about preservation and renovation," Davina stated. "But yes… I might just go back to Florida for a while."

"For the rest of your life," Ma said. "Go on with you. You're in love and I'm tired of seeing you walking around, pining away for that good-looking Italian."

"Do you think I should?" she asked Ma and Darren.

"Yes," they both said.

"Yes." Tilly's reply came from the kitchen.

Then her brother Quinn, who was now officially done with his tour of duty, walked in, his blue eyes bright, his dark hair a little longer now, and said, "Yes, please." Tugging someone else into the room, he said, "'Cause if you don't go to Florida, I think we might have a houseguest for a long, long time."

Davina dropped her hammer. "Santo?"

"I came to help," he said with a shrug. "And I brought a few of my friends with me."

She watched in awe as Alec, Blain, Rory and Hunter all stalked in. "We're reporting for work, boss."

Davina's gaze met Santo's. He was carrying a familiar box.

"I know where you got those and I hope you're willing to share," she said, eyeing the cupcake emblem.

"That depends," Santo said. "I have stipulations."

"I'm pretty sure this man loves you," Tilly said. "That's his stipulation. What are you waiting for?"

Davina gulped in a breath and rushed into

Santo's arms. "I love him, too," she said. "I do. I love this man." Then she snatched the box away from him with a grin.

"It's about time," Darren said, pride in the words. "And yes, we could use some help here."

Davina shooed her brother away while she kissed the man she loved. "I don't know what I was thinking, trying to stay away from you."

"You were trying to be a good daughter," he said. "But I need you to be my wife. Our children are waiting for you."

"I like the sound of that," she replied. "Help me here and feed me a cupcake and I promise I will follow you home."

"That sounds like a plan," he said. Then he kissed her while their fascinated audience clapped and whooped.

"C'mon, it's almost time for the Fourth of July fireworks," Gabby called out, her great-aunt Hattie's hand in hers.

"We have plenty of time," Marla said, grinning over at her husband. "Before we watch the show, I'd like to thank Santo and Davina for hosting this party. Santo, your new home is so lovely. Welcome to the neighborhood."

Santo smiled and lifted his cup of soda. "Glad to be here. And I should be able to spend more time here since I have a very capable new assistant to help me at work."

Annette Pickett had finally showed up at his office one day and told him how sorry she was about making things harder for him. "I heard about what you'd been through with your children and how you wanted to start a new life and I just ignored all that and I judged you way too harshly. But after talking to Preacher Rory and some other friends, I realized I'd been so wrong to judge you. I want to start over, too. Preacher Rory has helped me and now my son has found a great place to teach him and show him the right path and...well, I'm blessed. I want to stop all of this so it won't be too late for Beatrice. I need a good job. I'm willing to give it a try if you are."

Santo had agreed. Best decision he'd ever made. Other than asking Davina to marry him. "Thank you all for coming," he said as he glanced around. "I'm blessed to have all of you in my life." He winked at Rikki.

Marla and Alec held each other and smiled. Roxie sat at Gabby's feet, waiting for a treat, and Angus lay on a rug in the corner, snoozing. Blain and Rikki were happy in their new cottage on the lake. Rory and Vanessa traveled back and forth to the girls' home she'd opened in Alabama and helped hundreds of troubled teens find hope again. Kandi Jordan, the foster teen Vanessa had first mentored, planned to work there after college. Hunter and Chloe led a life of mystery and danger, solving corporate crimes. And Santo and Davina were going to get married this Christmas and make their hectic schedule work since they'd soon have offices side-by-side at Alvanetti Imports. He was content at last.

"So…we have an announcement," he said, smiling at Davina. Her whole family was here also and Nancy Connell gave him a thumbs-up. "We're going to get married."

"We've already figured that one out," Alec said on a droll note. But everyone congratulated them and hugged them anyway.

Then Alec held up his hand again. "Marla and I have one more announcement and then it's on to fireworks."

"What?" Gabby asked, looking between them. "Y'all are already married."

"Yes, we are," Alec replied. "Thank goodness."

"We're going to have a baby," Marla said, bending down to smile at Gabby. "How would you like that?"

Gabby clapped her hands. "You mean, a brother or sister, all for me?"

"Yes, all for you," Marla said, tears in her eyes. "For all of us."

Santo hugged Davina close while everyone celebrated. "This is amazing," he said. "I've lived here all my life but right now in this very minute, I finally feel as if I belong."

"You do belong," she said, touching a hand to his face. "To me. And now you have my family and all of these other people in your life."

"And us."

They turned to find his mother and father standing there. After hugs and introductions, Franco Alvanetti stated, "We're tired of traveling." He hugged his grandchildren tight. "We missed all of you."

"We're home for good," Sonia said, hugging Rikki and Santo and giving her grandchildren kisses. "And we want details on all of this."

"Yes, you've got a lot of explaining to do," Franco Alvanetti said in his gruff voice, his dark eyes full of pride.

"Yes, I do," Santo admitted. "I'll tell you all about it after the fireworks."

His father chuckled and patted him on the back. "I love this house, son."

"So do I," Santo replied. "And I love the woman who restored both this house and me."

Franco inclined his head toward Davina. "So I hear."

Taking Davina by the hand, Santo said, "Let's go watch the fireworks."

"Good idea." She kissed his cheek. "But I have a feeling they're just beginning."

* * * * *

Dear Reader,

I hope you enjoyed this last installment of the Men of Millbrook Lake. I had not expected to write a fifth book, but after Santo showed up in Book Two (*Her Holiday Protector*), I knew he had to have his own book. I wanted this solemn, stoic man to have his own happily-ever-after. There are a lot of hurting people in the world who deal with loved ones who've taken the wrong path. Sometimes that path leads to tragedy. Santo's story is about how to deal with the worst kind of tragedy—betrayal and death.

He needed a woman like Davina who could show him the true meaning of family. While they come from different backgrounds, they had that love of family in common. We can all learn a lesson from their issues.

I will miss my Men of Millbrook Lake but I hope you will continue to follow them and tell your friends about them. They will always hold a special place in my heart because they kept me busy while I adjusted to a new life in the beautiful state of Florida.

Until next time,
May the angels watch over you. Always.
Lenora

LARGER-PRINT BOOKS!

**GET 2 FREE
LARGER-PRINT NOVELS
PLUS 2 FREE
MYSTERY GIFTS**

Love Inspired®

SUSPENSE
RIVETING INSPIRATIONAL ROMANCE

Larger-print novels are now available…

YES! Please send me 2 FREE LARGER-PRINT Love Inspired® Suspense novels and my 2 FREE mystery gifts (gifts are worth about $10). After receiving them, if I don't wish to receive any more books, I can return the shipping statement marked "cancel." If I don't cancel, I will receive 4 brand-new novels every month and be billed just $5.49 per book in the U.S. or $5.99 per book in Canada. That's a savings of at least 19% off the cover price. It's quite a bargain! Shipping and handling is just 50¢ per book in the U.S. and 75¢ per book in Canada.* I understand that accepting the 2 free books and gifts places me under no obligation to buy anything. I can always return a shipment and cancel at any time. Even if I never buy another book, the two free books and gifts are mine to keep forever.

110/310 IDN GH6P

Name	(PLEASE PRINT)
Address	Apt. #
City	State/Prov.	Zip/Postal Code

Signature (if under 18, a parent or guardian must sign)

Mail to the Reader Service:
IN U.S.A.: P.O. Box 1867, Buffalo, NY 14240-1867
IN CANADA: P.O. Box 609, Fort Erie, Ontario L2A 5X3

**Are you a current subscriber to Love Inspired® Suspense books
and want to receive the larger-print edition?
Call 1-800-873-8635 or visit www.ReaderService.com.**

* Terms and prices subject to change without notice. Prices do not include applicable taxes. Sales tax applicable in N.Y. Canadian residents will be charged applicable taxes. Offer not valid in Quebec. This offer is limited to one order per household. Not valid for current subscribers to Love Inspired Suspense larger-print books. All orders subject to credit approval. Credit or debit balances in a customer's account(s) may be offset by any other outstanding balance owed by or to the customer. Please allow 4 to 6 weeks for delivery. Offer available while quantities last.

Your Privacy—The Reader Service is committed to protecting your privacy. Our Privacy Policy is available online at www.ReaderService.com or upon request from the Reader Service.

We make a portion of our mailing list available to reputable third parties that offer products we believe may interest you. If you prefer that we not exchange your name with third parties, or if you wish to clarify or modify your communication preferences, please visit us at www.ReaderService.com/consumerschoice or write to us at Reader Service Preference Service, P.O. Box 9062, Buffalo, NY 14240-9062. Include your complete name and address.

LISLP15

REQUEST YOUR FREE BOOKS!
2 FREE WHOLESOME ROMANCE NOVELS
IN LARGER PRINT
PLUS 2
FREE
MYSTERY GIFTS

✿ ✿ ✿ ✿ ✿ ✿ ✿ ✿ ✿ ✿ ✿ ✿ ✿ ✿ ✿ ✿ ✿ ✿ ✿

HEARTWARMING™
✿ ✿ ✿ ✿ ✿ ✿ ✿ ✿ ✿ ✿ ✿ ✿ ✿ ✿ ✿ ✿ ✿ ✿

Wholesome, tender romances

YES! Please send me 2 FREE Harlequin® Heartwarming Larger-Print novels and my 2 FREE mystery gifts (gifts worth about $10). After receiving them, if I don't wish to receive any more books, I can return the shipping statement marked "cancel." If I don't cancel, I will receive 4 brand-new larger-print novels every month and be billed just $5.24 per book in the U.S. or $5.99 per book in Canada. That's a savings of at least 19% off the cover price. It's quite a bargain! Shipping and handling is just 50¢ per book in the U.S. and 75¢ per book in Canada.* I understand that accepting the 2 free books and gifts places me under no obligation to buy anything. I can always return a shipment and cancel at any time. Even if I never buy another book, the two free books and gifts are mine to keep forever.

161/361 IDN GHX2

Name _____ (PLEASE PRINT) _____

Address _____ Apt. # _____

City _____ State/Prov. _____ Zip/Postal Code _____

Signature (if under 18, a parent or guardian must sign) _____

Mail to the **Reader Service:**
IN U.S.A.: P.O. Box 1867, Buffalo, NY 14240-1867
IN CANADA: P.O. Box 609, Fort Erie, Ontario L2A 5X3

* Terms and prices subject to change without notice. Prices do not include applicable taxes. Sales tax applicable in N.Y. Canadian residents will be charged applicable taxes. Offer not valid in Quebec. This offer is limited to one order per household. Not valid for current subscribers to Harlequin Heartwarming larger-print books. All orders subject to credit approval. Credit or debit balances in a customer's account(s) may be offset by any other outstanding balance owed by or to the customer. Please allow 4 to 6 weeks for delivery. Offer available while quantities last.

Your Privacy—The Reader Service is committed to protecting your privacy. Our Privacy Policy is available online at www.ReaderService.com or upon request from the Reader Service.

We make a portion of our mailing list available to reputable third parties that offer products we believe may interest you. If you prefer that we not exchange your name with third parties, or if you wish to clarify or modify your communication preferences, please visit us at www.ReaderService.com/consumerchoice or write to us at Reader Service Preference Service, P.O. Box 9062, Buffalo, NY 14240-9062. Include your complete name and address.

HW15

WESTERN WP PROMISES

YES! Please send me **The Western Promises Collection** in Larger Print. This collection begins with 3 FREE books and 2 FREE gifts (gifts valued at approx. $14.00 retail) in the first shipment, along with the other first 4 books from the collection! If I do not cancel, I will receive 8 monthly shipments until I have the entire 51-book Western Promises collection. I will receive 2 or 3 FREE books in each shipment and I will pay just $4.99 US/ $5.89 CDN for each of the other four books in each shipment, plus $2.99 for shipping and handling per shipment. *If I decide to keep the entire collection, I'll have paid for only 32 books, because 19 books are FREE! I understand that accepting the 3 free books and gifts places me under no obligation to buy anything. I can always return a shipment and cancel at any time. My free books and gifts are mine to keep no matter what I decide.

272 HCN 3070 472 HCN 3070

Name	(PLEASE PRINT)	
Address		Apt. #
City	State/Prov.	Zip/Postal Code
Signature (if under 18, a parent or guardian must sign)		

Mail to the **Reader Service:**
IN U.S.A.: P.O. Box 1867, Buffalo, NY 14240-1867
IN CANADA: P.O. Box 609, Fort Erie, Ontario L2A 5X3

* Terms and prices subject to change without notice. Prices do not include applicable taxes. Sales tax applicable in N.Y. Canadian residents will be charged applicable taxes. This offer is limited to one order per household. All orders subject to approval. Credit or debit balances in a customer's account(s) may be offset by any other outstanding balance owed by or to the customer. Please allow 4 to 6 weeks for delivery. Offer available while quantities last. Offer not available to Quebec residents.

WPBPA16R

READERSERVICE.COM

Manage your account online!

- Review your order history
- Manage your payments
- Update your address

> **We've designed the Reader Service website just for you.**

Enjoy all the features!

- Discover new series available to you, and read excerpts from any series.
- Respond to mailings and special monthly offers.
- Connect with favorite authors at the blog.
- Browse the Bonus Bucks catalog and online-only exculsives.
- Share your feedback.

Visit us at:

ReaderService.com